EVERLASTING ILLUSTRATED

I0016433

GREAT EXPECTATIONS

by
Charles Dickens

Original Novel abridged for
Modern Readers

LITTLE SCHOLARZ PVT LTD.
INDIA

This edition first originated and published in 2019

LITTLE SCHOLARZ Pvt Ltd.

12-H, New Daryaganj Road, Opp. Officers' Mess, New Delhi-110002 (India)
Phone # 91-11-23275124, 23275224, 23245124, 23261567
email : info@littlescholarz.com
website : www.littlescholarz.com
for online purchase : www.rameshpublishinghouse.com

© LITTLE SCHOLARZ Pvt. Ltd.

GREAT EXPECTATIONS

ISBN: 978-93-86063-44-1

HSN Code: 49011010

Book Code: S-434

Contents

❖ Chapter-1 ... 5

❖ Chapter-2 ... 8

❖ Chapter-3 ... 11

❖ Chapter-4 ... 12

❖ Chapter-5 ... 15

❖ Chapter-6 ... 18

❖ Chapter-7 ... 19

❖ Chapter-8 ... 22

❖ Chapter-9 ... 26

❖ Chapter-10 ... 27

❖ Chapter-11 ... 28

❖ Chapter-12 ... 33

❖ Chapter-13 ... 35

❖ Chapter-14 ... 38

❖ Chapter-15 ... 39

❖ Chapter-16 ... 41

❖ Chapter-17 ... 43

❖ Chapter-18 ... 45

❖ Chapter-19 ... 49

❖ Chapter-20 ... 51

❖ Chapter-21 ... 53

❖ Chapter-22 ... 55

❖ Chapter-23 ... 59

❖ Chapter-24 ... 60

❖ Chapter-25 ... 62

❖ Chapter-26 ... 64

❖ Chapter-27 ... 65

❖ Chapter-28 ... 67

❖ Chapter-29 ... 68

❖ Chapter-30 ... 74

❖ Chapter-31 ... 75

❖ Chapter-32 ... 78

❖ Chapter-33 ... 79

❖ Chapter-34 ... 81

❖ Chapter-35 ... 84

❖ Chapter-36 ... 85

❖ Chapter-37 ... 87

❖ Chapter-38 ... 90

❖ Chapter-39 ... 93

❖ Chapter-40 ... 99

❖ Chapter-41 ... 105

❖ Chapter-42 ... 107

❖ Chapter-43 ... 113

❖ Chapter-44 ... 114

❖ Chapter-45 ... 116

❖ Chapter-46 ... 118

❖ Chapter-47 ... 120

❖ Chapter-48 ... 121

❖ Chapter-49 ... 123

❖ Chapter-50 ... 125

❖ Chapter-51 ... 128

❖ Chapter-52 ... 129

❖ Chapter-53 ... 131

❖ Chapter-54 ... 135

❖ Chapter-55 ... 143

❖ Chapter-56 ... 145

❖ Chapter-57 ... 147

❖ Chapter-58 ... 150

❖ Chapter-59 ... 154

❖ Glossary ... 158
(word-meanings)

❖ Short and Long ... 159
Questions

❑❑❑

CHAPTER 1

My father's family name being Pirrip, and my Christian name Philip, my infant tongue could make of both names nothing longer or more explicit than Pip. So, I called myself Pip, and came to be called Pip.

Ours was the marsh country, down by the river, within, as the river wound, twenty miles of the sea. It was afternoon towards evening. I was in the church yard where my father, mother and five brothers were buried.

"Hold your noise!" cried a terrible voice, as a man started up from among the graves "or I'll cut your throat!"

A fearful man, all in coarse gray, with a great iron on his leg. A man with no hat, and with broken shoes, and with an old rag tied round his head. A man who had been soaked in water, and smothered in mud, and lamed

"Hold your noise!" cried a terrible voice.

by stones, and cut by flints, and stung by
nettles, and torn by briars; who limped, and
shivered, and glared, and growled; and whose
teeth chattered in his head as he seized me by
the chin.

He asked me my name and put me some
other questions.

Then, he said, "You get me a file." He tilted me again. "And you get me wittles."

"You bring 'em both to me."

"Or I'll have your heart and liver out."

I was dreadfully frightened.

He went on in these fearful terms :

"You bring me, to-morrow morning early, that file and the wittles. You bring the lot to me, at that old Battery over yonder." You do it, and you never dare to say a word or dare to make a sign concerning your having seen such a person as me, or any person sumever, and you shall be let to live."

I said that I would get him the file, and I would get him what broken bits of food I could, and I would come to him at the Battery, early in the morning.

"Say Lord strike you dead if you don't!" said the man.

I said so, and he took me down.

Then he limped towards the low church wall. I saw him go, picking his way among the nettles, and among the brambles that bound the green mounds.

❏❏❏

CHAPTER 2

My sister, Mrs. Joe Gargery, was more than twenty years older than I. She was not a good-looking woman, my sister; Joe was a fair man, with curls of flaxen hair on each side of his smooth face, and with eyes of a very undecided blue.

My sister, Mrs. Joe, with black hair and eyes, had a prevailing redness of skin. She was tall and bony, and almost always wore a coarse apron, fastened over her figure behind with two loops.

Joe's forge adjoined our house, which was a wooden house. When I ran home from the churchyard, the forge was shut up, and Joe was sitting alone in the kitchen.

"Where have you been, you young monkey?" said Mrs. Joe, as she saw me.

"I have only been to the churchyard," said I. My sister had a trenchant way of cutting our bread and butter for us, that never varied.

On the present occasion, though I was hungry, I dared not eat my slice.

I took advantage of a moment when Joe had just looked at me, and got my bread and butter down my leg.

It was Christmas Eve, and I had to stir the pudding for next day, with a copper-stick.

"Hark!" said I, "was that great guns, Joe?"

"Ah!" said Joe. "There's another convict off."
"What does that mean, Joe?" said I.

Mrs. Joe, said, snappishly, "Escaped. Escaped."

"There was a convict off last night," said Joe, aloud, "after sunset-gun. And they fired warning of him. And now it appears they're firing warning of another."

"Mrs. Joe," said I, "I should like to know— where the firing comes from?"

"From the Hulks!" said my sister.

"And please, what's Hulks?" said I.

"Hulks are prison-ships, right 'cross th' meshes," answered she.

"I wonder who's put into prison-ships, and why they're put there?" said I.

"People are put in the Hulks because they murder, and because they rob, and forge, and do all sorts of bad."

I was afraid to sleep, for I knew that at the first faint dawn of morning I must rob the pantry. There was no doing it in the night, for there was no getting a light by easy friction then; to have got one I must have struck it out of flint and steel, and have made a noise.

At day-break, I got up and went downstairs. In the pantry, I stole some bread, some rind of cheese, about half a jar of mincemeat, some brandy, a meat bone and a pork pie.

There was a door in the kitchen, communicating with the forge; I unlocked and unbolted that door, and got a file from among Joe's tools. Then I put the fastenings as I had found them, opened the door at which I had entered when I ran home last night, shut it, and ran for the misty marshes.

CHAPTER 3

I was getting on towards the river. I had just crossed a ditch when I saw the man sitting before me.

I went forward softly and touched him on the shoulder. He instantly jumped up, and it was not the same man, but another man!

And yet this man was dressed in coarse gray, too, and had a great iron on his leg, and was lame, and hoarse, and cold.

I was soon at the Battery after that, and there was the right Man,—waiting for me. I handed him all that I had brought.

Then I told him about the other man I had seen. But he was down on the rank wet grass, filing at his iron like a madman, and not minding me or minding his own leg.

⅂⅂⅂

CHAPTER 4

No discovery had yet been made of the robbery. Mrs. Joe was prodigiously busy in getting the house ready for the festivities of the day.

Mr. Wopsle, the clerk at church, was to dine with us; and Mr. Hubble the wheelwright and Mrs. Hubble; and Uncle Pumblechook (Joe's uncle), who was a well-to-do cornchandler in the nearest town, and drove his own chaise-cart. Joe and I had gone to church. When we got home, we found the table laid. And still, not a word of the robbery. Soon the company came.

"Have a little brandy, uncle," said my sister.

O Heavens, it had come at last! He would find it was weak, and I was lost!

My sister went for the stone bottle, came back with the stone bottle, and poured his brandy out: no one else taking any. The

I opened the door to the company.

wretched man trifled with his glass, took it up, looked at it through the light, put it down, prolonged my misery.

Instantly afterwards, the company were seized with unspeakable consternation, owing to his springing to his feet, turning round several times in an appalling spasmodic whooping-cough dance, and rushing out at the door.

I had filled up the bottle from the tar-water jug. Somehow he was brought back. Then, Uncle Pumblechook, asked for hot gin and water. So for the time being at least, I was saved.

"You must taste," said my sister, addressing the guests with her best grace—"you must taste, to finish with, such a delightful and delicious present of Uncle Pumblechook's!"

"You must know," said my sister, rising, "it's a pie; a savory pork pie."

The company murmured their compliments. My sister went out to get it. I heard her steps proceed to the pantry. I could bear no more, and ran for my life.

But I ran no farther than the house door, for there I ran head-foremost into a party of soldiers with their muskets, one of whom held out a pair of handcuffs to me, saying, "Here you are, look sharp, come on!"

ᄀᄀᄀ

CHAPTER 5

The coming of a file of soldiers, caused the dinner-party to rise from table in confusion, and caused Mrs. Joe re-entering the kitchen empty-handed, lamenting, What's gone—with the—pie! However, the sergeant wanted a pair of handcufts to be repaired immediately.

Joe said that it would take nearer two hours.

I was beginning to perceive that the handcuffs were not for me.

At last, Joe's job was done. Then, Mr Wopsle and Joe along with me accompanied the soldiers.

Now, I feared if convicts were there, they might think that it was I who had brought the soldiers there.

The soldiers were moving on in the direction of the old Battery, and we were moving on a little way behind them, when, all of a sudden, we all stopped. For there had reached us on the wings of the wind and rain, a long shout. It was repeated. We moved in the direction of shouting.

As we came nearer to the shouting, we saw two men struggling at the bottom of a ditch.

Both were bleeding and panting and execrating and struggling; but of course I knew them both directly.

"Mind!" said my convict, wiping blood from his face with his ragged sleeves, and shaking torn hair from his fingers: "I took him! I give him up to you! Mind that!"

The other convict was livid to look at, and, in addition to the old bruised left side of his face, seemed to be bruised and torn all over. He could not so much as get his breath to speak, until they were both separately handcuffed, but leaned upon a soldier to keep himself from falling.

"Take notice, guard,—he tried to murder me," were his first words.

"All right," said the sergeant. "March."

The two were kept apart, and each walked surrounded by a separate guard.

After an hour or so of this travelling, we came to a rough wooden hut and a landing-place. There the sergeant made some kind of report, and some entry in a book, and then the convict whom I call the other convict was drafted off with his guard, to go on board first.

My convict never looked at me, except that once. Suddenly, he turned to the sergeant, and remarked,—

"You know, a man can't starve; at least I can't. I stole some wittles, up at the village over yonder. From the blacksmith's. It was some broken wittles—that's what it was—and a dram of liquor, and a pie."

"Have you happened to miss such an article as pie, blacksmith?" asked the sergeant.

"My wie did, at the very moment when you came in. Don't you know, Pip?"

"So", said my convict, turning his eyes on Joe in a moody manner, and without the least glance at me,—" so you're the blacksmith, are you? Than I'm sorry to say, I've eat your pie."

"God knows you're welcome to it," returned Joe.

CHAPTER 6

I loved Joe,—perhaps for no better reason in those early days than because the dear fellow let me love him.

It was much upon my mind (particularly when I first saw him looking about for his file) that I ought to tell Joe the whole truth. Yet I did not, for I feared losing Joe's confidence.

As I was sleepy before we were far away from the prison-ship, Joe took me on his back again and carried me home.

I found Joe telling them about the convict's confession, and all the visitors suggesting different ways by which he had got into the pantry.

ᘯᘯᘯ

CHAPTER 7

When I was old enough, I was to be apprenticed to Joe.

Mr. Wopsle's great-aunt kept an evening school in the village. She rented a small cottage, and Mr. Wopsle had the room upstairs.

Mr. Wopsle's kept in the same room—a little general shop. It was Biddy who arranged all the shop transaction. Biddy was Mr. Wopsle's great-aunt's granddaughter. She was an orphan like myself; like me, too, had been brought up by hand.

Mainly with the help of Biddy, I struggled through the alphabet letters.

One night I, with great efforts, wrote a letter to Joe. It read:—

"MI DEER JO i OPE U R KR WITE WELL i OPE i SHAL SON B HABELL 4 2 TEEDGE

"Pip, old chap! What a scholar you are!"

U JO AN THEN WE SHORL B SO GLODD
AN WEN i M PRENGTD 2 U JO WOT LARX
AN BLEVE ME INF XN PIP."

Joe received it as a miracle of erudition.

"I say, Pip, old chap!" cried Joe, opening his
blue eyes wide, "what a scholar you are! An't
you?"

Mrs. Joe who had gone out come on a mare said, "Miss Havisham wants this boy to go and play there. And of course he's going."

I had heard of Miss Havisham up town, everybody for miles round had heard of Miss Havisham up town,—as an immensely rich and grim lady who lived in a large and dismal house barricaded against robbers, and who led of life of seclusion.

"Well to be sure!" said Joe, as tounded. "I wonder how she come to know Pip!"

"And couldn't she ask Uncle Pumblechook if he knew of a boy to go and play there?" said Mrs Joe. "Isn't it just barely possible that Uncle Pumblechook may be a tenant of her?"

"We can tell," she said, "This boy's fortune may be made by his going to Miss Havisham's. Uncle Pumblechook has offered to take him into town to-night in his own chaise-cart, and to keep him to-night, and to take him with his own hands to Miss Havisham's to-morrow morning."

I was then delivered over to Mr. Pumblechook.

"Good-bye, Joe!" said I.

CHAPTER 8

We started at ten o'clock and within a quarter of an hour we came to Miss Havisham's house, which was of old brick, and dismal, and had a great many iron bars to it.

The door was opened by a pretty young lady, Estella, who was very proud and scorned at me. I was taken in but Mr. Pumblechook, was asked to go back.

I learnt from the girl that one of the names of the place was the Manor House.

"One more. Its other name was Satis," she said, "for enough."

Though she called me "boy" she was of about my own age.

At last we came to the door of a room, and she said, "Go in."

I found myself in a pretty large room, well lighted with wax candles. No glimpse of daylight was to be seen in it. It was a dressing-room, as I supposed from the furniture. But prominent in it was a draped table with a gilded looking-glass, and that I made out at first sight to be a fine lady's dressing-table.

In an arm-chair, with an elbow resting on the table and her head leaning on that hand, sat the strangest lady I have ever seen, or shall ever see.

She was dressed in rich materials,—satins, and lace, and silks,—all of white. Her shoes were white. And she had a long white veil dependent from her hair, and she had bridal flowers in her hair, but her hair was white.

Some bright jewels sparkled on her neck and on her hands, and some other jewels lay sparkling on the table. Dresses, less splendid than the dress she wore, and half-packed trunks, were scattered about.

She had not quite finished dressing, for she had but one shoe on,—the other was on the table near her hand,—her veil was but half arranged, her watch and chain were not put on, and some lace for her bosom lay with those trinkets, and with her handkerchief, and gloves, and some flowers, and a Prayer-Book all confusedly heaped about the looking-glass.

I noted that both her watch, and the clock in the room had stopped at twenty minutes to nine.

"Look at me," said Miss Havisham. "You are not afraid of a woman who has never seen the sun since you were born?"

I regret to state that I had to say "No."

"Do you know what I touch here?" she said, laying her hands, one upon the other, on her left side. "Yes, ma'am. Your heart."

"Broken!"

"I am tired," said Miss Havisham. "I want diversion, and I have done with men and women. Play."

Then she called Estella, and said to her, "Let me see you play cards with this boy."

"With this boy? Why, he is a common laboring boy!"

I thought I overheard Miss Havisham answer,—"Well? You can break his heart."

"What do you play, boy?" asked Estella.

"Nothing but beggar my neighbor, miss."

"Beggar him," said Miss Havisham to Estella.

We sat down to cards. She won the game, and I dealt. I misdealt, as was only natural, and she denounced me for a stupid, clumsy laboring-boy.

I played the game to an end with Estella, and she beggared me. She threw the cards down on the table when she had won them all, as if she despised them for having been won of me.

"There, there! I know nothing of days of the week; I know nothing of weeks of the year. Come again after six days."

"Estella, take him down. Let him have something to eat, and let him roam and look about him while he eats. Go, Pip."

I was fed like a dog. After some time I saw Estella approaching with the keys, to let me out.

"Why don't you cry?" she said

"Because I don't want to."

"You do," said she. "You have been crying till you are half blind, and you are near crying again now".

*C*HAPTER 9

When I reached home, my sister was very curious to know all about Miss Havisham's, and asked a number of questions. Then that bullying old Pumblechook, came.

They sat debating what results would come to me from Miss Havisham's acquaintance.

And then I told Joe that I felt very miserable. There had been a beautiful young lady at Miss Havisham's who was dreadfully proud, and that she had said I was common.

"There's one thing you may be sure of, Pip," said Joe, "namely, that lies is lies. You are oncommon in some things. Likewise you're a oncommon scholar. Even a king must have started at A and worked his way to Z when he was a prince."

It rather encouraged me. Joe was however sorry when he learnt that there were no flags.

CHAPTER 10

In order to become uncommon I requested Biddy to impart all her learning to me. Biddy, who was the most obliging of girls, immediately agreed.

One evening I visited the public-house Three Jolly Bargemen, to call Joe, as directed by my sister. There I found Joe in company with Mr. Wopsle and a stranger.

I learnt from their talk that Mr Jaggers was his name. After talking about runaway convicts, Joe told Mr Jaggers about me.

Before leaving, the stranger gave me a shilling wrapped in some crumpled paper.

On reaching home, I took it out of the paper. "But what's this?" said Mrs. Joe, throwing down the shilling and catching up the paper. "Two One-Pound notes?"

CHAPTER 11

At the appointed time I returned to Miss Havisham's, and my hesitating ring at the gate brought out Estella.

There was a clock in the outer wall of this house. Like the clock in Miss Havisham's room, and like Miss Havisham's watch, it had stopped at twenty minutes to nine. Estella made me stand in a corner outside a gloomy room.

There were three ladies in the room and one gentleman. They somehow conveyed to me that they were all toadies and had come that day being the birthday of Miss Havisham.

One of the ladies was Camilla. The name of another lady was Sarah Pocket and the third lady was Estella. The name of the gentleman was Cousin Raymond.

After a short while Estella came.

"So, are you ready to play?"

We were soon in Miss Havisham's room. Estella left me standing near the door, and I stood there until Miss Havisham cast her eyes upon me from the dressing-table, and said.

"So, are you ready to play?"

"I don't think I am, ma'am," said I.

"Not at cards again?" she demanded.

"Yes, ma'am; I could do that, if I was wanted."

"If you are unwilling to play, are you willing to work?" she asked.

I said I was quite willing.

"Then go into that opposite room," said she, "and wait there till I come."

From that room, too, the daylight was completely excluded, and it had an airless smell that was oppressive. Certain wintry branches of candles on the high chimney-piece faintly lighted the chamber. The most prominent object was a long table with a tablecloth spread on it, as if a feast had been in preparation when the house and the clocks all stopped together. A centre-piece of some kind was in the middle of this cloth; it was so heavily overhung with cobwebs.

I was watching crawling things in the room when Miss Havisham came. In her other hand she had a crutch-headed stick on which she leaned and she looked like the Witch of the place.

"This," said she, pointing to the long table with her stick, "is where I will be laid when I am dead."

"What do you think that is?" she asked me, again pointing with her stick; "that, where those cobwebs are?"

"I can't guess what it is, ma'am."

"It's a great cake. A bride-cake. Mine!"

She looked all round the room, "Come, come, come! Walk me, walk me!"

I made out from this, that the work I had to do, was to walk Miss Havisham round and round the room.

After a while she said, "Call Estella!"

Estella brought with her the three ladies and the gentleman whom I had seen below.

They tried to make much of Miss Havisham, but she hardly showed any interest in their flattering talks.

At length, not coming out of her distraught state by degrees, but in an instant.

Miss Havisham said, "Let me see you two play cards, why have you not begun?" With that, we returned to her room, and sat down as before; I was beggared, as before; and again, as before, Miss Havisham watched us all the time, directed my attention to Estella's beauty, and made me notice it the more by trying her jewels on Estella's breast and hair.

Estella, for her part, likewise treated me as before, except that she did not condescend to speak. When we had played some half-dozen games, a day was appointed for my return, and I was taken down into the yard to be fed in the former dog-like manner. There, too, I was again left to wander about.

As I looked in at a window, I found myself, exchanging a broad stare with a pale young gentleman with red eyelids and light hair.

"Come and fight," said the pale young gentleman.

In his most mechanical fight with me he got mauled badly, and fell unconscious.

Then Estella called me.

"Come here! You may kiss me, if you like," she said.

I kissed her cheek as she turned it to me. It was night when I reached home.

CHAPTER 12

I felt that the pale young gentleman's blood was on my head, and that the Law would avenge it. For some days, I even kept close at home. I tried to wash out that evidence of my guilt in the dead of night.

I even thought Miss Havisham, preferring to take personal vengeance for an outrage done to her house, might rise in those grave-clothes of hers, draw a pistol, and shoot me dead.

However, go to Miss Havisham's I must, and go I did. And no pale young gentleman was to be discovered on the premises.

On the broad landing between Miss Havisham's own room and that other room in which the long table was laid out, I saw a garden-chair,—a light chair on wheels, that you pushed from behind. It had been placed there since my last visit, and I entered, that same day, on a regular occupation of pushing Miss Havisham in this chair (when she was tired of walking with her hand upon my shoulder) round her own room, and across the landing, and round the other room.

Over and over again, we would make these journeys, and sometimes they would last as long as three hours at a stretch. It was settled that I should return every alternate day at noon for these purposes.

However, she offered me no support and gave me no money but only my daily dinner.

Estella was always about. Her moods towards me changed frequently. Miss Havisham watched her moods and whispered to her, "Break their hearts my pride and hope, break their hearts and have no mercy!"

I reposed complete confidence in no one but Biddy; and I told her everything.

One day Miss Havisham said to me.

"You are growing tall, Pip!"

She advised me to get apprenticed at once. She asked me to bring Joe Gargery to her with my indentures.

Chapter 13

The next day but one, Joe accompanied me to Miss Havisham's. Estella opened the gate as usual. She told me we were both to go in. Miss Havisham was seated at her dressing-table, and looked round at us immediately.

"Oh!" said she to Joe. "You are the husband of the sister of this boy?"

"Well!" said Miss Havisham. "And you have reared the boy, with the intention of taking him for your apprentice?"

"You know, Pip," replied Joe, "as you and me were ever friends, and it were looked forward to betwixt us, Not but what, Pip, if you had ever made objections to the business?"

"Has the boy," said Miss Havisham, "ever made any objections? Does he like the trade?"

"Which it is well beknown to yourself, Pip," returned Joe, "that it were the wish of your own hart."

"Pip has earned premium here," said Miss Havisham.

"Have you brought his indentures with you?" asked Miss Havisham.

Joe took them out from his hat and gave them, not to Miss Havisham, but to me. I took the indentures out of his hand and gave them to Miss Havisham.

"Pip has earned a premium here," Miss Havisham said, "and here it is. There are five-and-twenty guineas in this bag. Give it to your master, Pip."

"Good by, Pip! You need not come again, Gargery is your master now," said Miss Havisham. "Let them out, Estella."

"Gargery! One word!"

"The boy has been a good boy here, and that is his reward. Of course, as an honest man, you will expect no other and no more."

The Justices were sitting in the Town Hall near at hand, and we at once went over to have me bound apprentice to Joe in the Magisterial presence.

Here, in a corner my indentures were duly signed and attested, and I was "bound".

We went back to Pumblechook's. And there my sister said that we must have a dinner out of that windfall at the Blue Boar.

❐❐❐

Chapter 14

The places like the best parlour, kitchen and forge had been lovable to me. Home had never been a very pleasant place to me, because of my sister's temper. But, Joe had sanctified it, and I had believed in it. Within a single year all this was changed. Now it was all coarse and common, and I would not have had Miss Havisham and Estella see it on any account.

How much of my ungracious condition of mind may have been my own fault, how much Miss Havisham's, how much my sister's, is now of no moment to me or to any one. The change was made in me; the thing was done.

Once, it had seemed to me that when I should at last roll up my shirt-sleeves and go into the forge, Joe's 'prentice, I should be distinguished and happy. Now the reality was in my hold, I only felt that I was dusty with the dust of small-coal. ❑❑❑

CHAPTER 15

Joe thought that if I were not received with cordiality, then this experimental trip should have no successor. By these conditions I promised to abide.

Now, Joe kept a journeyman at weekly wages whose name was Orlick. He pretended that his Christian name was Dolge.

He had the habit of slouching and slouching out wherever he went out.

This morose journeyman had no liking for me. When I became Joe's 'prentice, he was perhaps confirmed in some suspicion that I should displace him.

The next when I reminded Joe of my half-holiday to visit Miss Havisham, he too demanded one. Then said Joe, "let it be a half-holiday for all."

On hearing it my sister was very angry. Then there was an exchange of hot words between the journeyman and my sister.

At this, Joe knocked down Orlick. I went upstairs to dress myself.

I went to Miss Havisham. She asked me whether I was looking round for Estella. "Abroad," said she; "educating for a lady; prettier than ever. Do you feel that you have lost her?" She spared me the trouble of considering, by dismissing me.

As I was loitering along the High Street, I met Mr. Wopsle. It was a very dark night when I set out with Mr. Wopsle on the walk home. Beyond town, we came upon Orlick.

As Mr. Wopsle and I reached home, we learnt that the house had been violently entered when Joe Gargery was out.

We made no stop until we got into our kitchen. It was full of people. So I became aware of my sister,—lying without sense or movement on the bare boards where she had been knocked down by a tremendous blow on the back of the head, dealt by some unknown hand when her face was turned towards the fire.   ☐☐☐

CHAPTER 16

I learnt that when Joe came home, he found her struck down on the floor.

He found her struck down on the floor.

Nothing had been taken away from any part of the house. But, there was one remarkable piece of evidence on the spot. On the ground beside her, was a convict's leg-iron which had been filed asunder.

My sister lay very ill in bed. Her sight, hearing power and even memory were impaired. But I kept my slate always by her, that she might indicate in writing what she could not indicate in speech. We were at a loss to find a suitable attendant for her, until Biddy became a part of our establishment.

Again and again and again, my sister had traced upon the slate, a character that looked like a curious T, which meant hammer.

At last, "Why, of course!" cried Biddy. "It's him!"

Orlick, without a doubt! She had lost his name, and could only signify him by his hammer.

After that day, a day rarely passed without her drawing the hammer on her slate, and without Orlick's slouching in and standing doggedly before her.

ᄀᄀᄀ

CHAPTER 17

Imperceptibly I became conscious of a change in Biddy, however. Her shoes came up at the heel, her hair grew bright and neat, her hands were always clean. She was not beautiful, —she was common, and could not be like Estella,—but she was pleasant and wholesome and sweet-tempered and had thoughtful, pretty eyes.

"Biddy," said I, after binding her to secrecy, "I want to be a gentleman."

"O, I wouldn't, if I was you!" she returned.

Then I told her about Estella, saying, "I want to be a gentleman on her account."

Biddy was the wisest of girls, and she tried to reason no more with me. She was vaguely convinced that I was very much ill-used by somebody, or by everybody.

We talked a good deal as we walked, and all that Biddy said seemed right. Biddy was never insulting, or capricious, or Biddy today and somebody else to-morrow.

When we came near the churchyard, from somewhere there started up, Old Orlick.

Biddy was much against his going with us, and said to me in a whisper, "Don't let him come; I don't like him, because he likes me—and dances over me whenever he catches my eye."

I kept an eye on Orlick after that night, and, whenever circumstances were favorable to his dancing at Biddy, got before him to obscure that demonstration. He had struck root in Joe's establishment, by reason of my sister's sudden fancy for him, or I should have tried to get him dismissed.

Now I was clear that Biddy was immeasurably better than Estella, and that the plain honest working life to which I was born had nothing in it to be ashamed of, but offered me sufficient means of self-respect and happiness.

CHAPTER 18

It was in the fourth year of my apprenticeship to Joe, and it was a Saturday night. There was a group assembled round the fire at the Three Jolly Bargemen, attentive to Mr. Wopsle as he read the newspaper aloud. Of that group I was one.

Then, and not sooner, I became aware of a strange gentleman leaning over the back of the settle opposite me, looking on.

"From information I have received," said the strange gentleman, "I have reasons to believe there is a blacksmith among you, by name Joseph—or Joe—Gargery. Which is the man?" "Here is the man," said Joe.

Then the strange gentleman said, "You have an apprentice."

"I am here!" I cried. I recognized him as the gentleman I had met on the stairs, on

*Mr. Wopsle read the newspaper to a
group assembled round the fire*

the occasion of my second visit to Miss
Havisham.

"My name," strange gentleman said, "is
Jaggers, and I am a lawyer in London.

"Now, Joseph Gargery, I am the bearer of
an offer to relieve you of this young fellow
your apprentice. You would not object to cancel

his indentures at his request and for his good? You would want nothing for so doing?" "The answer is," returned Joe, sternly, "No."

"Now, I return to this young fellow. And the communication I have got to make is, that he has Great Expectations.

"I am instructed to communicate to him," said Mr. Jaggers, "that he will come into a handsome property. Further, that it is the desire of the present possessor of that property, that he be immediately removed from his present sphere of life and from this place, and be brought up as a gentleman,—in a word, as a young fellow of great expectations."

My dream was out; Miss Havisham was going to make my fortune on a grand scale.

"Now, Mr. Pip," pursued the lawyer, first, that it is the request of the person from whom I take my instructions that you always bear the name of Pip. If you have any objection, this is the time to mention it." I said excitedly, "No."

He further said, "Now, Mr. Pip, the name of the person who is your liberal benefactor remains a profound secret, until the person chooses to reveal it."

"Now, Mr. Pip, there is already lodged in my hands a sum of money amply sufficient for your suitable education and maintenance. You will please consider me your guardian. Now, there is a certain tutor, of whom I have some knowledge, who I think might suit you," said Mr. Jaggers. "The gentleman I speak of is one Mr. Matthew Pocket."

Ah! I caught at the name directly. Miss Havisham's relation.

"Good. You had better try him in his own house. The way shall be prepared for you, and you can see his son first, who is in London. When will you come to London?"

"First," said Mr. Jaggers, "you should have some new clothes to come in, and they should not be working-clothes." He gave me twenty guineas for this purpose.

He then delivered his valedictory remarks.

"Well, Mr. Pip, I think the sooner you leave here—as you are to be a gentleman—the better. You can take a hackney-coach at the stage-coach office in London, and come straight to me."

CHAPTER 19

After breakfast, Joe brought out my indentures from the press in the best parlor, and we put them in the fire, and I felt that I was free.

I went circuitously to Miss Havisham's by all the back ways, and rang the bell. Sarah Pocket came to the gate.

"I am going to London, Miss Pocket," said I, "and want to say good bye to Miss Havisham."

She went to ask if I were to be admitted. After a very short delay, she returned and took me up. Miss Havisham was taking exercise in the room with the long spread table, leaning on her crutch stick.

"Don't go, Sarah," she said. "Well, Pip?"

"I start for London, Miss Havisham, tomorrow," I was exceedingly careful what I said, "and I thought you would kindly not mind my taking leave of you."

"This is a gay figure, Pip," said she.

"I have come into such good fortune since I saw you last, Miss Havisham," I murmured. "And I am so grateful for it, Miss Havisham!"

"Ay, ay!" said she, "I have seen Mr. Jaggers. I have heard about it, Pip, and have got some details about it."

"Well" she went on; "you have a promising carrer before you. Be good—deserve it—and abide by Mr. Jagger's instructions. Good by, Pip!"

She stretched out her hand, and I went down on my knee and put it to my lips.

I was to leave our village at five in the morning, and I had told Joe that I wished to walk away all alone.

Biddy was astir so early to get my breakfast. It was a hurried breakfast.

"Well! I suppose I must be off!", said I and then I kissed my sister, and kissed Biddy, and threw my arms around Joe's neck. Then I took up my little portma-nteau and walked out.

⊐⊐⊐

CHAPTER 20

It was a little past midday when the four-horse stage-coach by which I was a passenger, got into the ravel of traffic frayed out about the Cross Keys, Wood Street, Chea-pside, London.

Mr. Jaggers had duly sent me his address; it was, Little Britain.

The coach stopped in a gloomy street, at certain offices with an open door, whereon was painted MR. JAGGERS. I went into the front office and asked, "Is Mr. Jaggers at home?" "He is not," returned the clerk. "He is in Court at present. Am I addressing Mr. Pip?" "Mr. Jaggers left word, would you wait in his room?"

After disposing of some other cases in the court, my guardian took me into his own room and informed me what arrangements he had made for me.

I was to go to "Barnard's Inn," to young Mr. Pocket's rooms, where a bed had been sent in for my accommodation; I was to remain with young Mr. Pocket until Monday; on Monday I was to go with him to his father's house on a visit, that I might try how I liked it.

Also, I was told what my allowance was to be,—it was a very liberal one,—and had handed to me from one of my guardian's drawers, the cards of certain tradesmen with whom I was to deal for all kinds of clothes, and such other things as I could in reason want.

"You will find your credit good, Mr. Pip," said my guardian, whose flask of sherry smelt like a whole caskful, as he hastily refreshed himself, "but I shall by this means be able to check your bills, and to pull you up if I find you outrunning. Of course you'll go wrong somehow, but that's no fault of mine."

Then Mr Jaggers sent me with Mr. Wemmick to my destination.

ᄆᄆᄆ

CHAPTER 21

Casting my eyes on Mr. Wemmick as we went along, to see what he was like in the light of day, I found him to be a dry man, rather short in stature, with a square wooden face.

"Do you know where Mr. Mathew Pocket lives?" I asked Mr. Wemmick.

"Yes," said he, nodding in the direction. "At Hammersmith, west of London, say five miles," from here.

Shortly we reached the Barnard's Inn. I was surprised to find the place the dingiest collection of shabby buildings ever squeezed together in a rank corner. Mr. Wemmick led me into a corner and conducted me up a flight of stairs.

Then Mr. Wemmick went away. Shortly afterwards, Mr Pocket Jr. arrived.

"Pray come in," said Mr. Pocket, Junior. "I am sure I shall be very happy to show London

"And you," said I, "are the pale young gentleman!"

to you. As to our table, you won't find that bad, for it will be at your expense, such being Mr. Jaggers's directions. As to our lodging, it's not by any means splendid, because I have my own bread to earn." Then he said, "Lord bless me, you're the prowling boy!"

"And you," said I, "are the pale young gentleman!" ⊐⊐⊐

Chapter 22

Soon I learnt that Mr. Herbert Pocket was his name. "Miss Havisham had sent for me, to see if she could take a fancy to me. But she couldn't, said he.

Talking of Estella, Herbert said, "That girl's hard and haughty and capricious and has been brought up by Miss Havisham to wreak revenge on all the male sex."

"What relation is she to Miss Havisham?"

"None," said he. "Only adopted."

"Why should she wreak revenge on all the male sex? I asked.

"Dear me! It's quite a story, and shall be saved till dinner-time. By the way, How did you come there, that day?"

I told him, and he was attentive until I had finished, and then burst out laughing again.

"Mr. Jaggers is your guardian, I understand?" he went on. "He is Miss Havisham's man of business and solicitor, and has her confidence when nobody else has"

"He was so obliging as to suggest my father for your tutor, and he called on my father to propose it. My father is Miss Havisham's cousin."

"Would you mind Handel for a familiar name? There's a charming piece of music by Handel, called the Harmonious Blacksmith," he continued. "I should like it very much."

At dinner, I reminded Herbert of his promise to tell me about Miss Havisham.

"True," he replied. "I'll redeem it at once. Let me introduce the topic, Handel, by mentioning some table manners in the use of fork, knife and spoon in particular in vogue in London." "Now," he pursued, "concerning Miss Havisham. Miss Havisham, you must know, was a spoilt child. Her mother died when she was a baby. Her father was a country gentleman and was a brewer." "Well! Mr. Havisham was very rich and very proud."

"She had a half-brother. Her father privately married again—his cook. As the son grew a young man, he turned out riotous, extravagant, undutiful,—altogether bad. At last his father disinherited him; but he softened when he was dying, and left him well off, though not nearly so well off as Miss Havisham."

"Miss Havisham was now an heiress, and you may suppose was looked after as a great match. Her half-brother had now ample means again, but what with debts and what with new madness wasted them most fearfully again. It is suspected that he cherished a deep and mortal grudge against her as having influenced the father's anger."

"There appeared upon the scene—a certain man, who made love to Miss Havisham. She perfectly idolized him, and he got great sums of money from her, and he induced her to buy her brother out of a share in the brewery (which had been weakly left him by his father) at an immense price, on the plea that when he was her husband he must hold and manage it all. Your guardian was not at that time in Miss Havisham's counsels, and she was too haughty and too much in love to be advised by any one. My father warned her that she was doing too much for this man, and was placing herself too unreservedly in his power.

She took the first opportunity of angrily ordering my father out of the house, in his presence, and my father has never seen her since."

"The marriage day was fixed, the wedding dresses were bought, the wedding tour was planned out, the wedding guests were invited. The day came, but not the bridegroom. He wrote her a letter—Which she received, when she was dressing for her marriage at twenty minutes to nine at which she afterwards stopped all the clocks. I don't know why the marriage broke off."

"It has been supposed that the man to whom she gave her misplaced confidence acted throughout in concert with her half-brother; that it was a conspiracy between them; and that they shared the profits."

Then I asked him, what he was? He replied, "A capitalist,—an Insurer of Ships."

On Monday morning we took coach for Hammersmith and reached Mr. Pocket's house. Mrs. Pocket was sitting on a garden chair. "Mamma," said Herbert, "this is young Mr. Pip." Upon which Mrs. Pocket received me with amiable dignity.

CHAPTER 23

M<small>r.</small> Pocket was a young-looking man, in spite of his perplexities and his very gray hair. Mr. Pocket took me into the house and showed me my room: which was a pleasant one. He then introduced me to two of his other pupils Drummle and Startop.

Mr. and Mrs. Pocket had a toady neighbor; a widow lady of that highly sympathetic nature. This lady's name was Mrs. Coiler.

I learnt that Mr. Pocket had been educated at Harrow and at Cambridge.

It came to my knowledge, through what passed between Mrs. Pocket and Drummle while I was attentive to my knife and fork, spoon, glasses, and other instruments of self-destruction, that Drummle, whose Christian name was Bentley, was actually the next heir but one to a baronetcy. ⛶⛶⛶

CHAPTER 24

Mr. Pocket had been told by Mr. Jaggers that I was not designed for any profession,

"Wemmick! Take Mr. Pip's written order and pay him twenty pounds."

and that I should be well enough educated for my destiny so that I could "hold my own."

He advised my attending certain places in London, for the acquisition of such mere rudiments as I wanted.

It occurred to me that if I could retain my bedroom in Barnard's Inn, my life would be agreeably varied, while my manners would be none the worse for Herbert's society.

Mr. Pocket did not object to this arrangement, but urged that before any step could possibly be taken in it, it must be submitted to my guardian.

I felt that this delicacy arose out of the consideration that the plan would save Herbert some expense, so I went off to Little Britain and imparted my wish to Mr. Jaggers.

I told Mr. Jaggers that I wanted to buy the furniture now hired for me.

"Wemmick!" said Mr. Jaggers, "Take Mr. Pip's written order, and pay him twenty pounds."

CHAPTER 25

Bentley Drummle, was an extremely sulky fellow. He was heavy in figure, movement, and comprehension and was idle, proud, niggardly, reserved, and suspicious. He came of rich people down in Somersetshire.

Startop had been spoilt by a weak mother and kept at home when he ought to have been at school, but he was devotedly attached to her, and admired her beyond measure.

He had a woman's delicacy of feature, and was—"exactly like his mother." It was but natural that I should take to him much more kindly than to Drummle.

When I had been in Mr. Pocket's family a month or two, Mr. and Mrs. Camilla turned up. Camilla was Mr. Pocket's sister.

Georgiana, whom I had seen at Miss Havisham's on the same occasion, also turned up. She was a cousin,—an indigestive single woman. These people hated me and they held Mrs. Pocket in contempt.

One day Mr Wemmick took me to his dwelling at Walworth. There he introduced me to his aged parent, who was very glad to see me. Wemmick also showed me his curiosities, prepared by him and his parent. I was well looked after there.

The supper was excellent; and though the Castle was rather subject to dry-rot insomuch that it tasted like a bad nut, and though the pig might have been farther off, I was heartily pleased with my whole entertainment. I was glad to learn that his dwelling was his own and was freehold. I stayed there for the night.

Wemmick was up early in the morning, and I am afraid I heard him cleaning my boots. After that he fell to gardening, and I saw him from my gothic window pretending to employ the Aged, and nodding at him in a most devoted manner. Our breakfast was as good as the supper, and at half-past eight precisely we started for Little Britain.

Chapter 26

My guardian was in his room, washing his hands with his scented soap, when I went into the office from Walworth. He gave me the invitation for myself and friends. "Come here tomorrow, and I'll take you home with me."

I learnt that he would wash his hands, whenever he came in from a police court or dismissed a client from his room.

He conducted us to Gerrard Street, Soho, to a house on the south side of that street.

Dinner was laid in the best of its rooms.

He had scarcely seen my three companions until now. To my surprise, he seemed to be principally if not solely interested in Drummle, whom he called "The spider".

In about a month after that, the Spider's time with Mr. Pocket was up for good. ❏❏❏

CHAPTER 27

I received a letter from Biddy announcing that Joe was coming to London along with Mr. Wopsle at a show as the latter had left the church and started play acting. I heard the avenging boy—announce "Mr. Gargery!" and he came in.

He reported about Mrs. Joe and Biddy. All tis time his eyes were rolling round the room.

I took what Joe gave me, and found it to be the crumpled play-bill of a small metropolitan theatre, announcing the first appearance, in that very week, of "the celebrated Provincial Amateur of Roscian renown, whose unique performance in the highest tragic walk of our National Bard has lately occasioned so great a sensation in local dramatic circles.

I was a bit perflexed about his simple working dress. But Joe's honesty and beauty of soul shone in even his simplest dress, and he said, rising from his chair, "and, Pip, I wish you ever well and ever prospering to a greater and a greater height."

"But you are not going now, Joe?"

"Yes I am," said Joe.

"But you are coming back to dinner, Joe?"

"No I am not," said Joe.

Our eyes met, and all the "Sir" melted out of that manly heart as he gave me his hand.

He continued, "Pip, dear old chap, life is made of ever so many partings welded together, as I may say, and one man's a blacksmith, and one's a whitesmith, and one's a goldsmith, and one's a coppersmith. Divisions among such must come, and must be met as they come. If there's been any fault at all to-day, it's mine. You and me is not two figures to be together in London; And so GOD bless you, dear old Pip, old chap, GOD bless you!"

I had not been mistaken in my fancy that there was a simple dignity in him. The fashion of his dress could no more come in its way when he spoke these words than it could come in its way in Heaven. He touched me gently on the forehead, and went out. ⊐⊐⊐

Chapter 28

It was clear that I must repair to our town next day, and stay at Joe's.

At that time it was customary to carry the convicts down to the dock-yards by stage-coach. So, I had no cause to be surprised when Herbert, meeting me in the yard, came up and told me that there were two convicts going down with me.

There stood the man whom I had seen on the settle at the Three Jolly Bargemen on a Saturday night, and who had brought me down with his invisible gun!

The words I heard them interchange as I became conscious, were the words of my own thought, "Two One Pound notes."

I alighted as soon as we touched the town. As to the convicts, they went their way with the coach. ⊐⊐⊐

CHAPTER 29

I began to think about Miss Havisham, who had adopted Estella and practically me too. I began to dream of bringing sunshine into her house and all that, and marrying Estella.

I loved Estella simply because I found her irresistible. It was early in the morning. As I rang the bell, I was surprised to see Orlick as, porter at Miss Havisham's door.

He took me in.

Then, I had gone up the staircase and tapped in my old way at the door of Miss Havisham's room. "Pip's rap," I heard her say, immediately; "come in, Pip."

She was in her chair near the old table. Sitting near her, was an elegant lady whom I had never seen.

The lady whom I had never seen before, was actually Estella. But she was so much

*I was surprised to see Orlick as porter at
Miss Havisham' door.*

changed, was so much more beautiful, so much
more womanly, in all things winning
admiration.

"Do you find her much changed, Pip?" asked
Miss Havisham.

"Yes," I replied.

"Is he changed?" Miss Havisham asked her.

"Very much," said Estella, looking at me.

"Less coarse and common?" said Miss Havisham.

"Yes," she replied.

I learnt that she had but just come home from France, and that she was going to London.

It was settled that I should stay there all the rest of the day, and return to the hotel at night, and to London tomorrow. When we had conversed for a while, Miss Havisham sent us two out to walk in the neglected garden: on our coming in by and by, she said, I should wheel her about a little, as in times of yore.

I told her that Herbert, the pale young gentleman was now my friend, and that his father was my tutor.

"Since your change of fortune and prospects, you have changed your companions," said Estella.

In my conscience, I doubt very much whether I had any lingering intention left of going to see Joe; but if I had, this observation put it to flight.

"You must know," said Estella, "that I have no heart."

I had gone up the staircase and tapped at the door of Miss Havisham's room.

Then she added, "Oh! I have a heart to be stabbed in or shot in," said Estella, "But you know what I mean. I have no softness there, no—sympathy—sentiment—nonsense."

"Let us make one more round of the garden, and then go in," she said.

At last we went back into the house, and there I heard, with surprise, that my guardian had come down to see Miss Havisham on business, and would come back to dinner.

Then, Estella being gone, Miss Havisham turned to me, and said in a whisper,—

"Is she beautiful, graceful, well-grown? Do you admire her?"

"Everybody must who sees her, Miss Havisham."

She drew my head close down to hers. "Love her, love her, love her!"

Then she added : "Hear me, Pip! I adopted her, to be loved."

"I'll tell you," she went on, "what real love is. It is blind devotion, unquestioning self-humiliation, utter submission, trust and belief against yourself and against the whole world, giving up your whole heart and soul to the smiter—as I did!"

As I drew her down into her chair, I saw my guardian in the room.

He always carried a pocket-handkerchief of rich silk and of imposing proportions, which was of great value to him in his profession. I have seen him to terrify a client or a witness by ceremoniously unfolding this pocket-handkerchief as if he were immediately going to blow his nose.

Miss Havisham had seen him as soon as I, and was (like everybody else) afraid of him.

Now, we were at the dinner-table, where she and Sarah Pocket awaited us. Mr. Jaggers presided Estella sat opposite to him, I faced green and yellow friend.

Then we played until nine o'clock, and then it was arranged that when Estella came to London I should be forewarned of her coming and should meet her at the coach; and then I took leave of her, and touched her and left her.

Far into the night at the Boar, Miss Havisham's words, "Love her, love her, love her!" sounded in my ears.

ᄀᄀᄀ

$\mathcal{C}$HAPTER 30

After visiting Miss Havisham, I had spent the night at the Blue Boar. After dinner I told Herbert that I loved Estella.

During the conversation with Herbert, I learnt that he was engaged to a girl, Clara, who lived in London.

As I put my hands in my pockets, I found the play-bill I had received from Joe, relative to the celebrated provincial amateur of Roscian renown. "And bless my heart," I involuntarily added aloud, "it's to-night!"

This changed the subject in an instant, and made us hurriedly resolve to go to the play. When Herbert had told me that his affianced already knew me by reputation and that I should be presented to her, we locked our door, and issued forth in quest of Mr. Wopsle and Denmark.

Chapter 31

On our arrival in Denmark, we found the king and queen of that country elevated in two arm-chairs on a kitchen-table, holding a Court. The whole of the Danish nobility were in attendance.

While certain events went on, upon my unfortunate townsman all the incidents accumulated with playful effect. Whenever that undecided Prince had to ask a question or state a doubt, the public helped him out with it.

As for example; on the question whether 'twas nobler in the mind to suffer, some roared yes, and some no, and some inclining to both opinions said "Toss up for it." And I grieve to add that peals of laughter greeted Mr. Wopsle on every occasion.

But his greatest trials were in the churchyard, which had the appearance of a primeval forest.

*We had sat, feeling keenly for him,
but laughing nevertheless, from ear to ear.*

As Mr. Wopsle in a comprehensive black cloak, being descried entering at the turnpike, the gravedigger was admonished in a friendly way.

We had made some pale efforts in the beginning to applaud Mr. Wopsle; but they were too hopeless to be persisted in. Therefore we had sat, feeling keenly for him, but laughing, nevertheless, from ear to ear. When the tragedy was over, and he had been called for and hooted, I said to Herbert, "Let us go at once, or perhaps we shall meet him."

But, as while coming downstairs the dresser took us through a little dirty swing door.

We found Mr. Wopsle was divesting himself of his Danish garments.

"Gentlemen," said Mr. Wopsle, "I am proud to see you."

I invited Mr Wopsle to supper, and he went to Barnard's with us. He sat until two o'clock in the morning, reviewing his success and developing his plans.

Miserably I went to bed after all, and miserably thought of Estella, and miserably dreamed that my expectations were all cancelled, and that I had to give my hand in marriage to Herbert's Clara, or play Hamlet to Miss Havisham's Ghost, before twenty thousand people, without knowing twenty words of it.

ᗗᗗᗗ

One day, I received a note by the post. It was from Estella, who said, "I am to come to London the day after to-morrow by the midday coach."

My appetite vanished instantly, and I knew no peace or rest until the day arrived. While I was haunting the coach-office in Wood Street, Cheapside, when Wemmick ran against me. I explained that I was waiting to meet somebody who was coming up by coach, and I inquired after the Castle and the Aged. "Both flourishing thankye," said Wemmick.

Mr. Wemmick and I parted at the office in Little Britain, where suppliants for Mr. Jaggers's notice were lingering about as usual, and I returned to my watch in the street of the coach-office, with some three hours on hand.

At last I saw Estella's face at the coach window and her hand waving to me. ❑❑❑

CHAPTER 33

In her furred travelling-dress, Estella seemed more delicately beautiful than she had ever seemed yet, even in my eyes.

"I am going to Richmond," she told me. "Our lesson is, that there are two Richmonds, one in Survey and one in Yorkshire, and that mine is the Surrey Richmond. The distance is ten miles. I am to have a carriage, and you are to take me. This is my purse, and you are to pay my charges out of it. O, you must take the purse! We have no choice, you and I, but to obey our instructions."

"Where are you going to, at Richmond?" I asked Estella.

"I am going to live," said she further, "with a lady there, who has the power—of taking me about, and introducing me, and showing people to me and showing me to people."

The bill was paid and we got into our post-coach and drove away.

"I wonder Miss Havisham could part with you again so soon," said I.

"It is a part of Miss Havisham's plans for me, Pip," said Estella, with a sigh, as if she were tired; I am to write to her constantly and see her regularly and report how I go on,—I and the jewels, —for they are nearly all mine now."

We came to Richmond all too soon, and our destination there was a house by the green,—a staid old house.

I got into the carriage to be taken back to Hammersmith, and I got in with a bad heart-ache, and I got out with a worse heart-ache. At our own door, I found little Jane Pocket coming home from a little party escorted by her little lover; and I envied her little lover, in spite of his being subject to Flopson.

Mr. Pocket was out lecturing, for, he was a most delightful lecturer on domestic economy, and his treatises on the management of children and servants were considered the very best text-books on those themes. ⊐⊐⊐

CHAPTER 34

The influence of my expectations was not all good. I lived in a state of chronic uneasiness respecting my behavior to Joe. My conscience was not by any means comfortable about Biddy. When I woke up in the night,— like Camilla,—I used to think, with a weariness on my spirits, that I should have been happier and better if I had never seen Miss Havisham's face, and had risen to manhood content to be partners with Joe in the honest old forge.

Yet Estella was inseparable from all my restlessness and disquiet of mind. Now, concerning the influence of my positon on others, I was in no such dificulty, and so I perceived—that it was not beneficial to anybody, and, above all, that it was not beneficial to Herbert. My lavish habits led his easy

Bentley Drummle floundered about in a cab of his own.

nature into expenses that he could not afford, corrupted the simplicity of his life and disturbed his peace with anxieties and regrets.

At Startop's suggestion, we put ourselves down for election into a club called The Finches of the Grove: the members dined expensively once a fortnight, and quarrelled among themselves after dinner.

The Finches spent their money foolishly, and the first Finch I saw was Bentley Drummle, at that time floundering about town in a cab of his own.

In my confidence in my own resources, I would willingly have taken Herbert's expenses on myself; but Herbert was proud, and I could make no such proposal to him.

I would then take a sheet of paper, and prepare on it "Memorandum of Pip's debts"; with Barnard's Inn. Similarly, Herbert would also take a sheet of paper, and prepare, "Memorandum of Herbert's debts."

One evening I suddenly received a letter. It was signed Trabb & Co., and its contents were simply, that I was an honored sir, and that they begged to inform me that Mrs. J. Gargery had departed this life on Monday last at twenty minutes past six in the evening, and that my attendance was requested at the interment on Monday next at three o'clock in the afternoon.

⊓⊓⊓

CHAPTER 35

My sister's death began to haunt me night and day. I was seized with a violent indignation against the assailant. Joe was seated apart at the upper end of the room. Biddy, went quietly here and there, and was very helpful. My sister was laid quietly in the earth.

"Now, how are you going to live, Biddy?" I asked.

"I am going to try to get the place of mistress in the new school."

"I am not going to leave poor Joe alone," I said to Biddy. Early in the morning I was to go. "Good by, dear Joe!—No, don't wipe it off—for God's sake, give me your blackened hand!—I shall be down soon and often."

Biddy was waiting for me at the kitchen door, with a mug of new milk and a crust of bread.

CHAPTER 36

Herbert and I went on from bad to worse, in the way of increasing our debts.

Herbert himself had come of age eight months before me. As he had nothing else than his majority to come into, the event did not make a profound sensation in Barnard's Inn.

I had taken care to have it well understood in Little Britain when my birthday was.

In the outer office Wemmick offered me his congratulations, and motioned me with a nod into my guardian's room.

"Well, Pip," said he, "I must call you Mr. Pip to-day. Congratulations, Mr. Pip."

"What do you suppose," said Mr. Jaggers, you are living at the rate of?

I confessed myself quite unable to answer the question.

"Have-I—anything to receive, sir?"

On that, Mr. Jaggers said, "I thought we should come to it!" and called to Wemmick to give him that piece of paper. Wemmick appeared, handed it in, and disappeared.

"Your name occurs pretty often in Wemmick's cash-book; but you are in debt, of course? Now, unfold it and tell me what it is."

"This is a bank-note," said I, "for five hundred pounds."

"That is a bank-note," repeated Mr. Jaggers.

"It is a present to you on this day, in earnest of your expectations. And at the rate of that handsome sum of money per annum, and at no higher rate, you are to live until the donor of the whole appears. That is to say, you will now take your money affairs entirely into your own hands, and you will draw from Wemmick one hundred and twenty-five pounds per quarter, until you are in communication with the fountain-head, and no longer with the mere agent. As I have told you before, I am the mere agent. I execute my instructions, and I am paid for doing so."

CHAPTER 37

Deeming Sunday the best day for taking Mr. Wemmick's Walworth sentiments, I devoted the next ensuing Sunday afternoon to a pilgrimage to the Castle. I rang at the gate, and was admitted in a most pacific manner by the Aged.

I could not help, admiring the mechanical appliances announcing a person's coming installed there, which the Aged proudly declared, "My son made it."

I saw the first demonstration of this contrivance when Wemmick came home with a lady, Miss Skiffins, who worked in the post-office branch of the service. Then there were other appliances also for various purposes.

One day I went to Wemmick in his office, having received a note from him. The upshot was, that we found a worthy young merchant

I was admitted in a most pacific manner by the Aged.

or shipping-broker, not long established in business, who wanted intelligent help, and who wanted capital, and who in due course of time would want a partner.

Between him and me, secret articles were signed of which Herbert was the subject, and I paid him half of my five hundred pounds down, and engaged for sundry other payments: some, to fall due at certain dates out of my income: some, contingent on my coming into my property.

Miss Skiffins's brother conducted the negotiation. Wemmick pervaded it throughout, but never appeared in it.

The whole business was so cleverly managed, that Herbert had not the least suspicion of my hand being in it. I never shall forget the radiant face with which he came home one afternoon, and told me, as a mighty piece of news, of his having fallen in with one Clarriker (the young merchant's name), and of Clarriker's having shown an extraordinary inclination towards him, and of his belief that the opening had come at last.

That night I went to bed, to think that my expectations had done some good to somebody.

ךךך

CHAPTER 38

My spirit was always wandering, about the house where Estella lived. The lady with whom Estella was placed, Mrs. Brandley by name, was a widow. Mrs. Brandley had been a friend of Miss Havisham's before the time of her seclusion.

In Mrs. Brandley's house and out of Mrs. Brandley's house, I suffered every kind and degree of torture that Estella could cause me. She made use of me to tease other admirers.

She had admirers without end. No doubt my jealousy made an admirer of every one who went near her.

I saw her often at Richmond, I heard of her often in town, at picnics, fête days, plays, operas, concerts, parties, all sorts of pleasures, through which I pursued her,—and they were all miseries to me.

One day Estella took me to Satis House; There was no change in it.

"How does she use you, Pip;" Miss Havisham asked me, with her witch-like eagerness.

Miss Havisham had Estella's arm drawn through her own, and when Estella gradually began to detach herself, said Miss Havisham, "are you tired of me?"

"Only a little tired of myself," replied Estella, disengaging her arm.

Miss Havisham spoke several harsh words to her saying that she was cold to her.

"You should know," said Estella. "I am what you have made me. Take all the praise, take all the blame; take all the success, take all the failure; in short, take me."

Miss Havisham complained that Estella had no love in her heart for her. There was an exchange of hot words between them.

Then Miss Havisham had settled down among the faded bridal relics upon the floor.

I came out of the room silently. When I at last took courage to return to the room, I found Estella sitting at Miss Havisham's knee, taking up some stitches in one of those old articles of dress that were dropping to pieces. Afterwards, Estella and I played at cards.

Before we left next day, there was no revival of the difference between her and Estella, nor was it ever revived on any similar occasion.

I was beside myself with anger when on a certain occasion when the Finches were assembled in force, Drummle called upon the company to pledge him to "Estella!"

It was decided at last that if Mr. Drummle would bring a certificate from the lady, that he had her acquaintance, Mr. Pip must express his regret.

Next day Drummle appeared with a polite little avowal in Estella's hand, that she had had the honor of dancing with him several times. This left me no course but to regret.

I soon find out, that Drummle had begun to follow her, and that she allowed him to do it.

"Do you deceive and entrap him, Estella?" I asked her and she said, "Yes, and many others, all of them but you. Here is Mrs. Brandley. I'll say no more."

CHAPTER 39

I was three-and-twenty years of age. We had left Barnard's Inn more than a year ago, and lived in the Temple. Our chambers were in Garden-court, down by the river.

Mr. Pocket and I had for some time parted company as to our original relations, though we continued on the best terms. Business had taken Herbert on a journey to Marseilles. I was alone. I lived on the top floor.

On a stormy and wet night a man came to me. He was substantially dressed, roughly, like a voyager by sea. His age was about sixty. He was a muscular man, strong on his legs, but he was browned and hardened by exposure to weather.

He looked about him with the strangest air,— and he pulled off a rough outer coat, and his hat. Then, I saw that his head was furrowed

He was substantially dressed, roughly, like a voyager by sea.

and bald, and that the long iron-gray hair grew only on its sides.

"It's disapinting to a man," he said, "arter having looked for'ard so distant, and come so fur."

"I'm glad you've grow'd up, a game one! But don't catch hold of me. You'd be sorry arterwards to have done it."

I relinquished the intention he had detected, for I knew him! He was my convict. He raised my hands to his lips, kissed them.

"You acted noble, my boy," said he. "Noble, Pip! And I have never forgot it!"

"You are wet, and you look weary. Will you drink something before you go?" said I.

"I think, that I will drink afore I go."

I made him some hot rum and water. When at last I put the glass to him, I saw with amazement that his eyes were full of tears.

"How are you living?" I asked him.

"I've been a sheep-farmer, stock-breeder, other trades besides, away in the new world," said he; "many a thousand mile of stormy water off from this." "I hope you have done well?" "I've done wonderfully well."

I turned off to a point that had just come into my mind.

"Have you ever seen a messenger you once sent to me," I inquired, "he came faithfully, and he brought me the two one-pound notes. I was a poor boy then. But, like you, I have done well since, and you must let me pay them back. You can put them to some other poor boy's use."

I took out my purse, and separated two one-pound notes from its contents handed them over to him. He laid them one upon the other, set fire to them at the lamp, and dropped the ashes into the tray. "May I make so bold," he said then, "as ask you how you have done well."

I forced myself to tell him that I had been chosen to succeed to some property. "What property? Whose property?" said he.

I faltered again, "I don't know."

"Could I make a guess, I wonder," said the convict, "at your income since you come of age! As to the first figure now. Five?"

My heart beat like a heavy hammer. He went on, "There ought to have been some guardian, or such-like, whiles you was a minor. Some lawyer, maybe. As to the first letter of that lawyer's name now. Would it be J and might be Jaggers?" Then he also made a mention of Wemmick.

"Yes, Pip, dear boy, I've made a gentleman on you! It's me wot has done it! I swore that time, sure as ever I earned a guinea, that guinea should go to you. I swore arterwards, sure as ever I spec'lated and got rich, you should get rich. I lived rough, that you should live smooth; I worked hard, that you should be above work."

"Look'ee here, Pip. I'm your second father. You're my son,—more to me nor any son. I've put away money, only for you to spend."

"And, dear boy, how good looking you have growed! There's bright eyes somewheres—eh? Isn't there bright eyes somewheres, wot you love the thoughts on?"

"O Estella, Estella! They shall be yourn, dear boy, if money can buy 'em. Not that a gentleman like you, so well set up as you, can't win 'em off of his own game; but money shall back you! It was the money left me, and the gains of the first few year wot I sent home to Mr. Jaggers—all for you—when he first come arter you, agreeable to my letter."

"And then, dear boy, it was a recompense to me, look'ee here, to know in secret that I was making a gentleman."

"Where will you put me to sleep?" he asked. "My friend and companion," said I, "is absent;

you must have his room, and he won't come back to-morrow."

"Because, look'ee here, dear boy," he said, "caution is necessary."

"How do you mean? Caution?"

"By G——, it's Death! I was sent for life. I should of a certainty be hanged if took."

The wretched man, had risked his life to come to me. My first care was to close the shutters, so that no light might be seen from without, and then to close and make fast the doors.

When I awoke the clocks of the Eastward churches were striking five, and the wind and rain intensified the thick black darkness.

THIS IS THE END OF THE SECOND STAGE OF PIP'S EXPECTATIONS.

ꝺꝺꝺ

CHAPTER 40

So, I had to take precautions to ensure (so far as I could) the safety of my dreaded visitor; not to arouse suspicion, I announced in the morning that my uncle had unexpectedly come from the country.

This course I decided on while I was yet groping about in the darkness for the means of getting a light. Not stumbling on the means after all, I was fain to go out to the adjacent Lodge and get the watchman there to come with his lantern. Now, in groping my way down the black staircase I fell over a man crouching in a corner.

I ran to the Lodge and urged the watchman to come quickly. We examined the staircase from the bottom to the top and found no one there. On my asking the watchman told me that he had admitted at his gate three men who had dined out last night.

"Besides them three gentlemen that I have named, a stranger asked for you," said the watchman and left.

Later, the convict told me that he had assumed the name "Provis" on board, but his real name was Abel Magwitch.

I put a number of questions to know if somebody had accompained him but he said, "No". Then I asked him if he had been tried in London. He said, "the last time" and Mr Jaggers was for there.

After breakfast he brought out a short pipe from the pocket of his coat and began to belt at it.

"I mustn't see my gentleman a footing it in the mire of the streets; there mustn't be no mud on his boots. My gentleman must have horses, Pip! Horses to ride, and horses to drive, and horses for his servant to ride and drive as well," said he.

He took out of his pocket a great thick pocket-book, and tossed it on the table.

"There's something worth spending in that book, dear boy. It's yourn. All I've got ain't mine; it's yourn. I've come to the old country fur to see my gentleman spend his money like a gentleman."

"Stop!" said I, "I want to know how you are to be kept out of danger, how long you are going to stay, what projects you have."

His answer was vague. "What precautions can be taken against your being recognized and seized?" I asked.

He went on harping, "I was low; that's what I was; low. Look over it, dear boy."

"Is there no chance person who might identify you in the street?" said I.

"Well," he returned, "there ain't many." The danger did not seem great to him.

"And how long do you remain?"

"I'm not a going back. I've come for good."

"Where are you to live?" said I. "What is to be done with you? Where will you be safe?"

"Dear boy," he returned, "there's disguising wigs can be bought for money, and there's hair powder, and spectacles, and black clothes,— shorts and what not. As to the where and how of living, dear boy, give me your own opinions on it."

It appeared to me that I could do no better than secure him some quiet lodging hard by, of which he might take possession when Herbert returned: whom I expected in two or three days. That the secret must be confided to Herbert as a matter of unavoidable necessity.

"And even then, dear boy," said he, pulling a greasy little clasped black Testament out of his pocket, "we'll have him on his oath."

I next discussed with him what dress he should wear. It was with considerable difficulty that I won him over to the assumption of a dress more like a prosperous farmer's.

He was to remain shut up in the chambers while I was gone, and was on no account to open the door.

There being to my knowledge a respectable lodging-house in Essex Street, the back of which looked into the Temple, and was almost within hail of my windows, I first of all repaired to that house, and was so fortunate as to secure the second floor for my uncle, Mr. Provis. I then went from shop to shop, making such purchases as were necessary to the change in his appearance. This business transacted, I turned my face, on my own account, to Little Britain.

"Lord strike you dead if ever you split in any sumever."

Mr. Jaggers was at his desk, but, seeing me enter, got up immediately and stood before his fire.

"Now, Pip," said he, "be careful."

"I merely want, Mr. Jaggers," said I, "to assure myself that what I have been told is true. I have been informed by a person named

Abel Magwitch, that he is the benefactor so long unknown to me."

"That is the man," said Mr. Jaggers, "in New South Wales. And only he."

"But I always supposed it was Miss Havisham."

"Take nothing on its looks; take everything on evidence," said Mr Jaggers.

Next day the clothes I had ordered all came home, and he put them on. Whatever he put on, became him less (it dismally seemed to me) than what he had worn before. To my thinking, there was something in him that made it hopeless to attempt to disguise him.

Meanwhile, Herbert also returned. "Herbert, my dear friend," said I, "something very strange has happened. This is—a visitor of mine."

Coming forward, with his little clasped black book, said Provis to Herbert. "Take it in your right hand. Lord strike you dead on the spot, if ever you split in any way sumever! Kiss it!"

"Do so, as he wishes it," I said to Herbert. So, Herbert, looking at me with a friendly uneasiness and amazement, complied.

CHAPTER 41

It was midnight before I took him round to Essex Street, and saw him safely in at his own dark door. I took all other precautions that I considered necessary and whenever required.

Herbert received me with open arms, and I had never felt before so blessedly what it is to have a friend.

I told Herbert clearly that I could no longer accept all he wanted to make available to me horses, and carriages, and lavish appearances of all kinds.

I further told him that I had now no expectations—though heavily in debt, and I was fit for nothing.

Herbert tried to console me as I broke down.

"See, then," said Herbert; "think of this! He comes here at the peril of his life, for the realization of his fixed idea. In the moment of realization, after all his toil and waiting, you cut the ground from under his feet, destroy his idea, and make his gains worthless to him. By your being under the disappointment, he might put himself in the way of being taken."

I was so struck by the horror of this idea that would make me regard myself, in some sort, as his murderer.

"The first and the main thing to be done," said Herbert, "is to get him out of England. You will have to go with him, and then he may be induced to go."

To know his history we decided to ask him point blank at breakfast.

When he had made an end of his breakfast, I said to him,—

"After you were gone last night, I told my friend of the struggle that the soldiers found you engaged in on the marshes, when we came up. We want to know something about that man—and about you."

He took out his black pipe, looked round at us, and said what follows.

ꙮꙮꙮ

CHAPTER 42

"**D**ear boy and Pip's comrade. My life, in short, has been in jail and out of jail, as I got shipped off. I've been done everything to, pretty well—except hanged."

"I was a ragged little creetur as much to be pitied as ever I see, I got the name of being hardened, they measured my head, some on 'em,—they had better a measured my stomach. But what the Devil was I to do? I must put something into my stomach."

"Tramping, begging, thieving, working sometimes when I could,—a bit of a poacher, a bit of a laborer, a bit of a wagoner, a bit of a haymaker, a bit of a hawker, a deserting soldier and so on."

"At Epsom races, a matter of over twenty years ago, I got acquainted wi' a man whose skull I'd crack wi' this poker, if I'd got it on this hob. His right name was Compeyson; and that's the man, dear boy, what you see me a pounding in the ditch."

"He set up fur a gentleman, this Compeyson, and he'd been to a public boarding-school and had learning. He was a smooth one to talk. He was good-looking too. It was the night afore the great race, when I found him on the heath, in a booth that I know'd on. He appointed me for next night. Same place."

"So, I went to Compeyson next night, same place, and Compeyson took me on to be his man and pardner. And what was Compeyson's business in which we was to go pardners? Compeyson's business was the swindling, handwriting forging, stolen bank-note passing, and such-like. All sorts of traps as Compeyson could set with his head, and keep his own legs out of and get the profits from and let another man in for, was Compeyson's business."

"There was another in with Compeyson, as was called Arthur. Him and Compeyson had been in a bad thing with a rich lady some years afore, and they'd made a pot of money by it; but Compeyson betted and gamed, and he'd have run through the king's taxes. So, Arthur was a dying."

A woman awfully mad and all in white comes with a shroud.

"Arthur lived at the top of Compeyson's house and Compeyson kept a careful account agen him for board and lodging, in case he should ever get better to work it out. But Arthur soon settled the account."

"Then he got rid of him by making him sick psychologically through a clever trick, wherein at midnight a woman awfully mad and all in white comes with a shroud."

"Him and me was soon busy, and first he swore me (being ever artful) on my own book,—this here little black book, dear boy, what I swore your comrade on."

"This Compeyson planned, and I done. He got me into such nets as made me his black slave. I was always in debt to him, always under his thumb, always a working, always a getting into danger. I was tried, alone, for misdemeanor, while with Compeyson?"

"Me and Compeyson was both committed for felony,—on a charge of putting stolen notes in circulation,—and there was other charges behind. Compeyson says to me, 'Separate defences, no communication,' and that was all. And I was so miserable poor, that I sold all the clothes I had, except what hung on my back, afore I could get Jaggers."

"When we was put in the dock, I noticed first of all what a gentleman Compeyson looked, wi' his curly hair and his black clothes and his white pocket-handkercher, and what a common sort of a wretch I looked. When the prosecution opened and the evidence was put short, aforehand, I noticed how heavy it all bore on me, and how light on him. Compeyson got only seven years for being an educated, well-dressed, well-mannered gentleman. I got fourteen years for being iliterate for looking ruste besides, Compeyson had cleverly kept himself free from all Guilt."

"I had said to Compeyson that I'd smash that face of his, and I swore Lord smash mine! to do it. We was in the same prison-ship, but I couldn't get at him for long, though I tried. At last I came behind him and hit him on the cheek to turn him round and get a smashing one at him, when I was seen and seized. The black-hole of that ship warn't a strong one, to a judge of black-holes that could swim and dive. I escaped to the shore, and I was a hiding among the graves there, envying them as was in 'em and all over, when I first see my boy!"

He regarded me with a look of affection that made him almost abhorrent to me again, though I had felt great pity for him.

"By my boy, I was giv to understand as Compeyson was out on them marshes too. I hunted him down. I smashed his face. I was put in irons, brought to trial again, and sent for life. I didn't stop for life, dear boy and Pip's comrade, being here."

He wiped himself again, as he had done before, and then slowly took his tangle of tobacco from his pocket, and plucked his pipe from his buttonhole, and slowly filled it, and began to smoke.

'Is he dead?' I asked after a silence.

'Is who dead, dear boy?'

'Compeyson.'

'He hopes I am, if he's alive, you may be sure,' with a fierce look. 'I never heard no more of him.'

Herbert had been writing with his pencil in the cover of a book. He softly pushed the book over to me, as Provis stood smoking.

I read in it :

"Young Havisham's name was Arthur. Compeyson is the man who professed to be Miss Havisham's lover."

I shut the book and nodded slightly to Herbert, and put the book by; but neither of us said anything, and both looked at Provis as he stood smoking by the fire.

CHAPTER 43

Now, I feared that if Compeyson were alive and should discover his return, he could find the safe means of getting rid of an enemy by becoming an informer.

I said to Herbert that, before I could go abroad, I must see both Estella and Miss Havisham.

Next day I feigned that I was under a binding promise to go down to Joe; Provis was to be strictly careful while I was gone, and Herbert was to take the charge of him. I was to be absent only one night.

I set off by the early morning coach. I met Drummle, but we parted soon.

Just then, three farmers came, one of them probably Orlick.

CHAPTER 44

In the room where the dressing-table stood, I found Miss Havisham and Estella.

I said to Miss Havisham, "I have found out who my patron is. There are reasons why I must say no more of that. It is not my secret, but another's."

"Further, I should be false and base if I did not tell you, that you deeply wrong both Mr. Matthew Pocket and his son Herbert, if you suppose them to be otherwise than generous, upright, open, and incapable of anything designing or mean."

"What do you want for them?"

"Miss Havisham, if you would spare the money to do my friend Herbert a lasting service in life, but which from the nature of the case must be done without his knowledge, I could show you how."

"Why must it be done without his knowledge?" she asked,

"Because," said I, "I began the service myself, more than two years ago, without his knowledge, and I don't want to be betrayed. Why I fail in my ability to finish it, I cannot explain. It is a part of the secret which is another person's and not mine."

"What else?" she said.

"Estella," said I, turning to her now, "You know I love you. You know that I have loved you long and dearly." "I know," said I, "I have no hope that I shall ever call you mine."

"Is it not true," said I, "that Bentley Drummle is in town here, and pursuing you?"

She said, "Why not tell you the truth? I am going to be married to him."

"Estella, dearest Estella, do not let Miss Havisham lead you into this fatal step. Bestow yourself on some worthier person than Drummle."

As I reached the Whitefriars gate, the night-porter gave me a note. It was in Wemmick's writing,— "DON'T GO HOME."

*C*HAPTER 45

M r. Wemmick had conveyed the message to me not to go home. So, I went to see Wemmick.

The house with the bow-window, by the river-side.

"I accidentally heard, yesterday morning," said Wemmick, "that you at your chambers in Garden Court, Temple, were being watched."

When asked about Compeyson, he answered that he was living and was in London.

"Now," said Wemmick, "I went to Garden Court to find you; not finding you, I went to Clarriker's to find Mr. Herbert. And him I found.

"Mr. Herbert," continued Wemmick, "struck out a plan.. He mentioned to me as a secret, that he is courting a young lady who has, as no doubt you are aware, a bedridden Pa. Which Pa, lies a-bed in a bow-window where he can see the ships sail up and down the river."

Then Wemmick explained to me the whole plan of Herbert. "Now, it was done without you, and when, if any one was concerning himself about your movements, you must be known to be ever so many miles off. This diverts suspicion and confuses it," he said.

Chapter 46

Herbert's scheme for Provis's safe ouster had been planned. It was now going to be implemented.

Selecting from the few queer houses upon Mill Pond Bank a house with a wooden front and three stories of bow-window, I looked at the plate upon the door, and read there, Mrs. Whimple.

It was the house where Clara, Herbert's beloved, lived. "Clara has no mother of her own, Handel, and no relation in the world but old Gruffandgrim, I mean Mr. Barley," said Herbert.

Just then a very pretty, slight, dark-eyed girl of twenty or so came in and presented, blushing, as "Clara."

In his two cabin rooms at the top of the house, which were fresh and airy, I found Provis comfortably settled.

Suggested Herbert, "We are both good watermen, Handel, and could take him down the river ourselves when the right time comes. No boat would then be hired for the purpose, and no boatmen; that would save at least a chance of suspicion, and any chance is worth saving. Never mind the season; don't you think it might be a good thing if you began at once to keep a boat at the Temple stairs, and were in the habit of rowing up and down the river? You fall into that habit, and then who notices or minds? Do it twenty or fifty times, and there is nothing special in your doing it the twenty-first or fifty-first."

I liked this scheme, and Provis was quite elated by it. We agreed that it should be carried into execution.

When we got to the foot of the stairs, I asked Herbert whether he had preserved the name of Provis. He replied, certainly not, and that the lodger was Mr. Campbell.

Next day I set myself to get the boat. It was soon done, and I started giving practical shape to Herbert's suggestion. I always bore in mind that there was cause for alarm, as I could not get rid of the notion of being watched. ❑❑❑

CHAPTER 47

One afternoon, I came ashore at the wharf. I had pulled down as far as Greenwich with the ebb tide, and had turned with the tide. Both way, I had seen the signal in his window, All well.

Mr. Wopsle had not succeeded in reviving the Drama, but, on the contrary, had rather partaken of its decline. By and by, I roused myself, and went to the play.

Mr. Wopsle told me that he had seen one of the two convicts, whom we had chased, sitting behind me. He was Compeyson. This conversation threw me, into special and peculiar terror at Compeyson's having been behind me "like a ghost."

I told Herbert about it and we communi-cated it to Wemmick what I had that night found out, and to remind him that we waited for his hint.

CHAPTER 48

I had strolled up into Cheapside, when a large hand was laid upon my shoulder by some one overtaking me. It was Mr. Jagger's hand.

On his invitation, I dined with him. He handed me a note from Miss Havisham. She wanted me to see her on a little matter of business. I said that I would go tomorrow.

"So here's to Mrs. Bentley Drummle," said Mr. Jaggers, taking a decanter of choicer wine from his dumb-waiter.

She was at his elbow when he addressed her, putting a dish upon the table. As she withdrew her hands from it, she fell back a step or two, nervously muttering some excuse. And a certain action of her fingers, as she spoke, arrested my attention.

The action of her fingers was like the action of knitting. Her look was very intent. Surely,

I felt certain that this woman was Estella's mother.

I had seen exactly such eyes and such hands on a memorable occasion very lately!

He dismissed her, and she glided out of the room. But she remained before me as plainly as if she were still there. And I felt absolutely certain that this woman was Estella's mother.

CHAPTER 49

Putting Miss Havisham's note in my pocket, I went down again by the coach next day.

"I want," she said, "to pursue that subject you mentioned to me."

"So!" said she, "And how much money is wanting to complete the purchase?"

"Nine hundred pounds."

"If I give you the money for this purpose, but you will keep my secret?"

She turned her face to me for the first time, and, to my amazement, she dropped on her knees at my feet; with her folded hands raised to me.

"O!" she cried, despairingly. "What have I done! What have I done!"

"Whose child was Estella?" I asked.

"Mr. Jaggers brought her here. I told him that I wanted a little girl to rear and love, and save from my fate. One night he brought her here asleep, and I called her Estella."

"Might I ask her age then?"

"Two or three. She herself knows nothing, but that she was left an orphan and I adopted her."

So convinced I was of that woman's being her mother, that I wanted no evidence to establish the fact in my own mind.

I found, on questioning the servants, that Estella was in Paris, and I got a promise from the surgeon that he would write to her by the next post. Miss Havisham's family I took upon myself; intending to communicate with Mr. Matthew Pocket only, and leave him to do as he liked about informing the rest. This I did next day, through Herbert, as soon as I returned to town.

Towards midnight she began to wander in her speech; She first came, "I meant to save her from misery like mine." And then, "Take the pencil and write under my name, 'I forgive her!'" She never changed the order of these three sentences.

CHAPTER 50

"I sat with Provis last night, Handel, two good hours," said Herbert.

"He was very communicative last night, and told me more of his life. You remember his breaking off here about some woman that he had had great trouble with. It seems that the woman was a young woman, and a jealous woman, and a revengeful woman. Well, she murdered somebody and was tried for it, and Mr. Jaggers defended her, and the reputation of that defence first made his name known to Provis. It was another and a stronger woman who was the victim, and whom she throttled."

"Was the woman brought in guilty?"

"No; she was acquitted."

"This acquitted young woman and Provis had a little child; of whom Provis was exceedingly fond. On the evening of the very

She swore that she would destroy the child.

night when the object of her jealousy was strangled as I tell you, the young woman presented herself before Provis for one moment, and swore that she would destroy the child (which was in her possession), and he should never see it again; then she vanished."

"Did the woman keep her oath?"

"He says she did."

Now, pursued Herbert, "fearing he should be called upon to depose about this destroyed child, and so be the cause of her death, he hid himself (much as he grieved for the child), kept himself dark, as he says, out of the way and out of the trial, and was only vaguely talked of as a certain man called Abel, out of whom the jealousy arose. After the acquittal she disappeared, and thus he lost the child and the child's mother."

"That evil genius, Compeyson, knowing of all this kept him poorer and working him harder."

"Let me remember. It had happened some three or four years then," he said.

"The man we have in hiding down the river, is Estella's Father."

ᄀᄀᄀ

CHAPTER 51

I had known about the parentage of Estella. It was now necessary to convey the information to Mr. Jaggers. I decided to see him. After getting the cheque for nine hundred pounds for Herbert from Mr. Jaggers, I said to him, "I have seen Estella's mother."

"Yes?" said Mr. Jaggers.

Then I said, "I know her father too, and his name is Provis—from New South Wales."

"And on what evidence, Pip," asked Mr. Jaggers, "does Provis make this claim?"

"He does not make it," said I, "and has never made it, and has no knowledge or belief that his daughter is in existence."

Mr. Jaggers put Estella's case in the right legal perspective to me and told me that revealing the secret could be of no benefit to anybody. ❏❏❏

*C*HAPTER *52*

Having got the cheque, it was now a smooth walk to brighten the prospects of Herbert.

I received the following letter from Wemmick by the post.

"Burn this as soon as read. On Wednesday, you might do what you know of."

When I had shown this to Herbert, said he, "I know a better course than taking a Thames waterman. Take Startop. A good fellow, a skilled hand."

We found that a steamer for Hamburg was likely to suit our purpose best.

Those two should pull a pair of oars, we settled, and I would steer; Herbert should not come home to dinner before going to Mill Pond Bank that evening; that he should not go there at all to-morrow evening, Tuesday; that he should prepare Provis to come down to some stairs hard by the house, on Wednesday, when he saw us approach, and not sooner; that all the arrangements with him should be concluded that Monday night; and that he should be communicated with no more in any way, until we took him on board.

On opening the outer door of our chambers with my key, I found a letter in the box. Its contents were these:

"Come to the old marshes to-night at nine, by the limekiln. If you want information regarding your uncle Provis, you had much better come and tell no one, and lose no time. You must come alone. Bring this with you." Having hardly any time for consideration,— I resolved to go.

I left a note in pencil for Herbert. I had decided to hurry down and back, to ascertain for myself how Miss Havisham was faring.

It was dark before we got down, and the journey seemed long and dreary to me. I went to Satis House and inquired for Miss Havisham; she was still very ill, though considered something better.

CHAPTER 53

I had received a letter asking me to go to the marshes. So, I went. It was a dark night. I saw a light in the old sluice-house.

Looking in, I saw a lighted candle on a table. Suddenly, I was caught in a strong running noose, thrown over my head from behind.

Then a flare of light flashed up, and showed me Orlick seated and bending over the table.

As I watched him in silence, he took up a gun with a brass-bound stock.

"How dared you to come betwixt me and a young woman I liked?" he said.

"Now, I'm a going to have your life!"

He had been drinking, and his eyes were red and bloodshot.

He brought the bottle to his lips, and took a fiery drink from it; "Wolf!" said he, "Old

Orlick's a going to tell you somethink. It was you as did for your shrew sister."

"I come upon her from behind. It was you. You was favored. Now you pays for it."

"Wolf, I'll tell you something more. It was Old Orlick as you tumbled over on your stairs that night."

"When Old Orlick come for to hear that your uncle Provis had most like wore the leg-iron wot Old Orlick had picked up, filed asunder, on these meshes ever so many year ago, and wot he kep by him till he dropped your sister with it."

"Old Orlick knowed you was smuggling your uncle Provis away, Old Orlick's a match for you. There's them that's as good a match for your uncle Provis as Old Orlick has been for you."

Then, I saw in his hand a stone-hammer with a long heavy handle.

I shouted out with all my might.

In the same instant I heard responsive shouts, and saw Orlick emerge from a struggle of men, and fly out into the night.

In the same instant I heard responsive shouts.

I saw the face of Trabb's boy!

Then, I saw my supporter to be—

"Herbert! Great Heaven!"

"And our old comrade, Startop!"

"The time has not gone by. It is still Monday night, and you have all to-morrow, Tuesday, to rest in," said Herbert.

I learnt from him that I had in my hurry dropped the letter, open, in our chambers. So he and Startop arrived at the Blue Boar, and after Miss Havisham's, where they lost me.

Hereupon they went back to the hotel to refresh themselves. They met Trabb's Boy,—who had seen me passing from Miss Havisham's in the direction of my dining-place. Thus Trabb's boy became their guide, and with him they went out to the sluice-house, though by the town way to the marshes, which I had avoided.

When suddenly I cried out loudly, and he answered the cries, and rushed in, closely followed by the other two.

Wednesday being so close upon us, we determined to go back to London that night, three in the post-chaise; the rather, as we should then be clear away before the night's adventure began to be talked of.

Wednesday morning was dawning when I looked out of window.

"When it turns at nine o'clock," said Herbert, cheerfully, "look out for us, and stand ready, you over there at Mill."

ꓘꓘꓘ

CHAPTER 54

We loitered down to the Temple stairs. After a little show of indecision, we went on board and cast off; Herbert in the bow, I steering.

We went on board and cast off.

Our plan was this. The tide, beginning to run down at nine, and being with us until three, we intended still to creep on after it had turned, and row against it until dark.

We could choose one of the public houses a resting-place. There, we meant to lie by all night. The steamer for Hamburg and the steamer for Rotterdam would start from London at about nine on Thursday morning.

We went ahead among many skiffs and wherries briskly. Passing along several places, and sitting in the stern, I could see, with a faster beating heart, Mill Pond Bank and Mill Pond stairs.

We touched the stairs lightly for a single moment, and he was on board, and we were off again. He had a boat-cloak with him, and a black canvas bag; and he looked as like a river-pilot as my heart could have wished.

As the night was fast falling, Herbert and Startop plied their oars once more, and I looked out for anything like a house.

At this dismal time we were evidently all possessed by the idea that we were followed.

It was half-past one before we saw the steamer's smoke, and soon afterwards we saw

I saw a four-oared galley shoot out from under the bank.

behind it the smoke of another steamer. As they were coming on at full speed, we got the two bags ready, and took that opportunity of saying good by to Herbert and Startop.

We had all shaken hands cordially, when I saw a four-oared galley shoot out from under the bank but a little way ahead of us, and row out into the same track.

I called to Herbert and Startop to keep before the tide. I adjured Provis to sit quite still, wrapped in his cloak. Meantime the galley, which was very skilfully handled, had crossed us, let us come up with her, and fallen alongside. Of the two sitters one held the rudder-lines, the other sitter was wrapped up, much as Provis was.

Startop could make out, after a few minutes, which steamer was first, and gave me the word "Hamburg." I felt as if her shadow were absolutely upon us, when the galley hailed us. I answered.

"You have a returned Transport there," said the man who held the lines. "That's the man, wrapped in the cloak. His name is Abel Magwitch, otherwise Provis. I apprehend that man, and call upon him to surrender, and you to assist."

At the same moment, without giving any audible direction to his crew, he ran the galley abroad of us. They had pulled one sudden stroke ahead, had got their oars in, had run athwart us, and were holding on to our gunwale, before we knew what they were doing. In the same moment, I saw the steersman of the galley lay his hand on his prisoner's shoulder, and saw that both boats were swinging round with the force of the tide, and saw that all hands on board the steamer were running forward quite frantically. Still, in the same moment, I saw the prisoner start up, lean across his captor, and pull the cloak from the neck of the shrinking sitter in the galley. Still in the same moment, I saw that the face disclosed, was the face of the other convict of long ago.

Still, in the same moment, I saw the face tilt backward with a white terror on it that I shall never forget, and heard a great cry on board the steamer, and a loud splash in the water, and felt the boat sink from under me.

It was but for an instant that I seemed to struggle with a thousand mill-weirs and a thousand flashes of light; that instant past, I was taken on board the galley. Herbert was there, and Startop was there; but our boat was gone, and the two convicts were gone.

What with the cries aboard the steamer, and the furious blowing off of her steam, and her driving on, and our driving on, shore from shore; but the crew of the galley righted her with great speed.

Presently a dark object was seen in it, bearing towards us on the tide. The steersman held up his hand, and kept the boat straight and true before it. As it came nearer, I saw it to be Magwitch, swimming, but not swimming freely. He was taken on board, and instantly manacled at the wrists and ankles.

At length we gave it up, and pulled under the shore towards the tavern we had lately left, where we were received with no little surprise. Here I was able to get some comforts for Magwitch,—Provis no longer,—who had received some very severe injury in the chest, and a deep cut in the head.

He told me that he believed himself to have gone under the keel of the steamer, and to have been struck on the head in rising. The injury to his chest (which rendered his breathing extremely painful) he thought he had received against the side of the galley.

He added that he did not pretend to say what he might or might not have done to Compeyson, but that, in the moment of his laying his hand on his cloak to identify him, that villain had staggered up and staggered back, and they had both gone overboard together, when the sudden wrenching of him (Magwitch) out of our boat, and the endeavor of his captor to keep him in it, had capsized us.

He told me in a whisper that they had gone down fiercely locked in each other's arms, and that there had been a struggle under water, and that he had disengaged himself, struck out, and swum away.

The officer took charge of everything his prisoner had about him. So the pocket-book which had once been in my hands passed into the officer's. He further gave me leave to accompany the prisoner to London; but declined to accord that grace to my two friends.

The Jack at the Ship was instructed where the drowned man had gone down, and undertook to search for the body in the places where it was likeliest to come ashore. His interest in its recovery seemed to me to be much heightened when he heard that it had stockings on.

We remained at the public-house until the tide turned, and then Magwitch was carried down to the galley and put on board. Herbert and Startop were to get to London by land, as soon as they could. We had a doleful parting, and when I took my place by Magwitch's side,

I felt that that was my place henceforth while he lived.

For now, my repugnance to him had all melted away; and in the hunted, wounded, shackled creature who held my hand in his, I only saw a man who had meant to be my benefactor, I told him how grieved I was to think that he had come home for my sake.

"Dear boy," Magwitch said, "I'm quite content to take my chance. I've seen my boy, and he can be a gentleman without me."

I understood Wemmick's hint now. I foresaw that, being convicted, his possessions would be forfeited to the Crown.

"Lookee here, dear boy," said he "It's best as a gentleman should not be knowed to belong to me now. Only come to see me as if you come by chance alonger Wemmick. Sit where I can see you when I am swore to, for the last o' many times, and I don't ask no more."

"I will never stir from your side," said I, "when I am suffered to be near you. Please God, I will be as true to you as you have been to me!"

CHAPTER 55

Magwitch was taken to the Police Court next day for his trial at the next Sessions.

It was at this dark time of my life that Herbert returned home one evening, a good deal cast down, and said,—

"My dear Handel, I fear I shall soon have to leave you."

"We shall lose a fine opportunity if I put off going to Cairo, and I am very much afraid I must go, Handel, when you most need me."

"In this branch house of ours, Handel, we must have a clerk." And I hope it is not at all unlikely that he may expand into a partner. Now, Handel,—in short, my dear boy, will you come to me? Even Clara wishes that you should live with us."

I thanked her heartily, and I thanked him heartily, but said I could not yet make sure of joining him as he so kindly offered.

On the Saturday in that same week, I took my leave of Herbert,—as he sat on one of the seaport mail coaches. I went into a coffee-house to write a little note to Clara, telling her he had gone off, sending his love to her over and over again, and then went to my lonely home.

Wemmick was taking a holiday and he invited me to take of walk with him from eight to twelve. Wemmick said suddenly,—

"Halloa! Here's a church!"

"Halloa!" said he. "Here's a couple of pair of gloves! Let's put 'em on!"

Then I beheld the Aged enter at a side door, escorting a lady.

"Halloa!" said Wemmick. "Here's Miss Skiffins! Let's have a wedding."

I heard Wemmick say to himself, as he took something out of his waistcoat-pocket before the service began, "Halloa! Here's a ring!" I acted in the capacity of backer, or best-man, to the bridegroom; while the responsibility of giving the lady away devolved upon the Aged.

Chapter 56

Magwitch lay in prison very ill, during the whole interval between his committal for trial and the coming round of the Sessions. He had broken two ribs, wounded one of his lungs, and he breathed with great pain and difficulty, which increased daily.

Although I saw him every day, it was for only a short time; The trial was very short and very clear.

The appointed punishment for his return to the land that had cast him out, being Death, and his case being this aggravated case, he must prepare himself to Die.

I began that night to write out a petition to the Home Secretary of State, I wrote out other petitions to such men in authority as I hoped were the most merciful, and drew up one to the Crown itself.

For several days and nights after he was sentenced I took no rest except when I fell asleep in my chair, but was wholly absorbed in these appeals.

The daily visits I could make him were shortened now, and he was more strictly kept. The number of the days had risen to ten, when I saw a greater change in him than I had seen yet.

His eyes were turned towards the door, and lighted up as I entered.

"Thank'ee dear boy, thank'ee. God bless you! You've never deserted me, dear boy," he said.

"Dear Magwitch," said I.

"You had a child once, whom you loved and lost. She lived, and found powerful friends. She is living now. She is a lady and very beautiful. And I love her!"

With a last faint effort, he raised my hand to his lips. Then, he gently let it sink upon his breast again, with his own hands lying on it.

I knew there were no better words that I could say beside his bed, than "O Lord, be merciful to him a sinner!"

CHAPTER 57

Now that I was left wholly to myself, I gave notice of my intention to quit the chambers in the Temple as soon as my tenancy could legally determine, and in the meanwhile to underlet them. I was falling very ill.

I was arrested for my debt to a jeweller.

I was having strange thoughts and dreadful ... visions. Day and night every where I saw Joe.

I said, "O Joe, you break my heart! Look angry at me, Joe. Strike me, Joe. Tell me of my ingratitude. Don't be so good to me!"

"Dear old Pip, old chap," said Joe, "you and me was ever friends. And when you're well enough to go out for a ride—what larks!

"Which you meantersay, Pip, how long have your illness lasted, dear old chap?"

"Yes, Joe."

"It's the end of May, Pip. Tomorrow is the first of June."

"And have you been here all that time, dear Joe?"

"Pretty nigh, old chap. For, as I says to Biddy when the news of your being ill were brought by letter, which it were brought by the post, and being formerly single he is now married."

"It is so delightful to hear you, Joe! But I interrupt you in what you said to Biddy."

"Which it were," said Joe, "that how you might be amongst strangers, and that how you and me having been every friends, a visit at such a moment might not prove unacceptable.

And Biddy, her words were, 'Go to him, without loss of time.'

Then we started to talk about Miss Havisham who had died.

"Dear Joe, have you heard what becomes of her property?"

"Well, old chap," said Joe, "I meantersay she had tied it up, on Miss Estella, leaving a cool four thousand to Mr. Matthew Pocket."

When I got up in the morning, refreshed and stronger yet, I was full of my resolution to tell Joe all, without delay. I went to his room, and he was not there.

I hurried then to the breakfast-table, and on it found a letter. These were its brief contents.

"Not wishful to intrude I have departured fur you are well again dear Pip and will do better without JO.

"P.S. Ever the best of friends."

Enclosed in the letter, was a receipt for the debt and costs on which I had been arrested. I had never dreamed of Joe's having paid the money; but, Joe had paid it, and the receipt was in his name.

What remained for me now, but to follow him to the dear old forge, and there to have out my disclosure to him, and my penitent remonstrance with him, and there to relieve my mind and heart of that reserve. Secondly, which had begun as a vague something lingering in my thoughts, and had formed into a settled purpose?

The purpose was, that I would go to Biddy, and ask her to marry me.

Such was my purpose. After three days more of recovery, I went down to the old place, to put it in execution; and how I sped in it, is all I have left to tell.

CHAPTER 58

Early in the morning, I strolled round by Satis House. There were printed bills on the gate, announcing a sale by auction of the Household Furniture and Effects, next week. The House itself was to be sold as old building materials, and pulled down.

The schoolhouse where Biddy was mistress I had never seen; but, the little roundabout lane by which I entered the village, for quietness' sake, took me past it. I was disappointed to find that the day was a holiday; no children were there, and Biddy's house was closed.

But the house was not deserted, and the best parlor seemed to be in use, for there were white curtains fluttering in its window, and the window was open and gay with flowers. I went softly towards it, meaning to peep over the flowers, when Joe and Biddy stood before me, arm in arm.

"But dear Biddy, how smart you are!" said I.

"Yes, dear Pip."

"And Joe, how smart you are!"

"Yes, dear old Pip, old chap."

"It's my wedding-day!" cried Biddy, in a burst of happiness, "and I am married to Joe!"

"Dear Biddy," said I, "you have the best husband in the whole world, and, you couldn't love him better than you do."

"And, dear Joe, you have the best wife in the whole world, and she will make you as happy as even you deserve to be, you dear, good, noble Joe!"

"And Joe and Biddy both, as you have been to church to-day, and are in charity and love with all mankind, receive my humble thanks for all you have done for me, and all I have so ill repaid!

And when I say that I am going away within the hour, for I am soon going abroad, and that I shall never rest until I have worked for the money with which you have kept me out of prison, and have sent it to you, don't think, dear Joe and Biddy, that if I could repay it a thousand times over, I suppose I could cancel a farthing of the debt I owe you, or that I would do so if I could!"

They were both melted by these words, and both entreated me to say no more.

"O dear old Pip, old chap," said Joe. "God knows as I forgive you, if I have anythink to forgive!"

"Amen! And God knows I do!" echoed Biddy.

"Now let me go up and look at my old little room, and rest there a few minutes by myself. And then, when I have eaten and drunk with you, go with me as far as the finger-post, dear Joe and Biddy, before we say good by!"

I sold all I had, and put aside as much as I could, for a composition with my creditors,—who gave me ample time to pay them in full,—and I went out and joined Herbert. Within a month, I had quitted England, and within two months I was clerk to Clarriker and Co., and within four months I assumed my first undivided responsibility.

Many a year went round before I was a partner in the House; but I lived happily with Herbert and his wife, and lived frugally, and paid my debts, and maintained a constant correspondence with Biddy and Joe.

It was not until I became third in the Firm, that Clarriker betrayed me to Herbert; but he then declared that the secret of Herbert's partnership had been long enough upon his conscience, and he must tell it. So he told it, and Herbert was as much moved as amazed, and the dear fellow and I were not the worse friends for the long concealment.

I must not leave it to be supposed that we were ever a great House, or that we made mints of money. We were not in a grand way of business, but we had a good name, and worked for our profits, and did very well.

CHAPTER 59

For eleven years, I had not seen Joe nor Biddy with my bodily Eyes,—when, upon an evening in December, an hour or two after dark, I laid my hand softly on the latch of the old kitchen door and went in.

I was glad to see their child. "We giv' him the name of Pip for your sake, dear old chap," said Joe delighted, when I took another stool by the child's side. Biddy said to me, gently. "You must marry." "So Herbert and Clara say, but I don't think I shall, Biddy. I have so settled down in their home, that it's not at all likely. I am already quite an old bachelor."

"Dear Pip," said Biddy, "you are sure you don't fret for her?" "O no,—I think not, Biddy."

"Tell me as an old, old friend. Have you quite forgotten her? "My dear Biddy, I have forgotten nothing in my life that ever had a foremost place there, and little that ever had

"We giv' him the name of Pip for your sake, dear old chap."

any place there. But that poor dream, as I once used to call it, has all gone by, Biddy,—all gone by!"

Nevertheless, I knew, while I said those words, that I secretly intended to revisit the site of the old house that evening, alone, for her sake. Yes, even so. For Estella's sake. I had heard of her as leading a most unhappy life, and as being separated from her husband, who had used her with great cruelty. And I had heard of the death of her husband.

The early dinner hour at Joe's, left me abundance of time, to walk over to the old spot before dark.

There was no house now, no brewery, no building whatever left, but the wall of the old garden. The cleared space had been enclosed with a rough fence. A gate in the fence standing ajar, I pushed it open, and went in.

I was looking along the desolate garden walk, when I beheld a solitary figure in it. I knew it was Estella, and I cried out,—"Estella!" The freshness of her beauty was indeed gone, but its indescribable majesty and its indescribable charm remained.

We sat down on a bench that was near, and I said, "After so many years, it is strange that we should thus meet again, Estella, here where our first meeting was!" She said, "The ground belongs to me. It is the only possession I have not relinquished. Everything else has gone from me, little by little, but I have kept this. It was the subject of the only determined resistance I made in all the wretched years."

"Is it to be built on?" "At last, it is. I came here to take leave of it before its change. And you," she said, in a voice of touching interest to a wanderer,—"you live abroad still?"

We sat down on a bench that was near.

"Still." "And do well, I am sure?"

"Yes, I do well." During the conversation both of us got assured that we told each other in the heart as something sacred.

"Then be as considerate and good to me as you were, and tell me we are friends," she said. "We are friends," said I, rising and bending over her, as she rose from the bench.

"And will continue friends apart," said Estella. I took her hand in mine, and we went out of the ruined place; and, I saw no shadow of another parting from her.   ❏❏❏

GLOSSARY
(word-meanings)

1.	*Advantage*	=	benefit
2.	*Instantly*	=	immediately
3.	*Indicated*	=	showed
4.	*Toadies*	=	sycophants
5.	*Oppressive*	=	offensive
6.	*Prominent*	=	important
7.	*Ungracious*	=	unkind
8.	*Gloomy*	=	sad, dark
9.	*Admiration*	=	praise
10.	*Accumulated*	=	gathered
11.	*Considerable*	=	much
12.	*Revealed*	=	divulged
13.	*Certainly*	=	definitely
14.	*Emerged*	=	appeared
15.	*Evidence*	=	proof
16.	*Ascertain*	=	make certain
17.	*Aggravated*	=	worsened
18.	*Tendency*	=	inclination
19.	*Ample*	=	sufficient
20.	*Amazed*	=	surprised

Short Questions

1. Describe Pip's encounter with the fearful man.

2. Describe the party at Joe's house.

3. Describe the soldiers' visit to Joe's and the arrest of the two convicts.

4. Describe Pip's first visit to Miss Havisham.

5. Describe Joe's visit to Miss Havisham's and Pip's becoming an apprentice to him.

6. Describe the attack on Mrs. Joe.

7. Explain Pip's views about Biddy.

8. Why did Jaggers ask Pip to visit his office in London?

9. What did Mathew Pocket tell Pip about Miss Havisham?

10. Describe Mr. Wopsle's performance at the show.

11. Describe the exchange of harsh words between Estella and Miss Havisham.

12. Describe the story of Magwitch as told by himself to Pip.

13. How did Pip come to know about Estella's mother?

14. Describe the relationship between Provis and Estella.

15. How was Pip trapped by Orlick and how did the former get release from him?

Long Questions

1. Give a character-sketch of Miss Havisham.

2. Describe the relationship between Pip and Estella.

3. Give a character-sktech of Joe.

4. Write a note on female characters in the novel.

5. Give a description of villainous characters in the novel.

6. Give a character-sketch of Magwitch.

7. Describe what efforts were made to save the life of Magwitch and what happened to him finally?

8. Describe the relationship between Pip and Herbert.

9. Describe the fight between Magwitch (Provis) and Compeyson.

10. Why was Magwitch imprisoned and what finally became of him?

11. Write a note on the end of the novel.

❏❏❏